## Sisterly Love

Dane went for his gun. Longarm was only a half step behind the man and he clubbed Dane viciously behind his ear, dropping him to the floor, then grabbing his pistol.

Pearl had a stubby two-shot derringer and brought it up in a flash, firing at the sheriff, whose attention had been diverted. The first bullet from Pearl's little pistol exploded in the close confines of the office and Longarm threw himself at the woman as she unleashed her second shot toward the falling sheriff.

Longarm's open palm slapped the side of Pearl's lovely, hate-twisted face and sent her reeling backward. Hilda jumped between her sister and the gun that had suddenly materialized in Longarm's hand.

"No!" she cried as gunshots erupted out in the street. "Don't kill her!"

DI022654

SEP 2014

# DON'T MISS THESE
## ALL-ACTION WESTERN SERIES
### FROM THE BERKLEY PUBLISHING GROUP

**THE GUNSMITH by J. R. Roberts**

Clint Adams was a legend among lawmen, outlaws, and ladies. They called him . . . the Gunsmith.

**LONGARM by Tabor Evans**

The popular long-running series about Deputy U.S. Marshal Custis Long—his life, his loves, his fight for justice.

**SLOCUM by Jake Logan**

Today's longest-running action Western. John Slocum rides a deadly trail of hot blood and cold steel.

**BUSHWHACKERS by B. J. Lanagan**

An action-packed series by the creators of Longarm! The rousing adventures of the most brutal gang of cutthroats ever assembled—Quantrill's Raiders.

**DIAMONDBACK by Guy Brewer**

Dex Yancey is Diamondback, a Southern gentleman turned con man when his brother cheats him out of the family fortune. Ladies love him. Gamblers hate him. But nobody pulls one over on Dex . . .

**WILDGUN by Jack Hanson**

The blazing adventures of mountain man Will Barlow—from the creators of Longarm!

**TEXAS TRACKER by Tom Calhoun**

J.T. Law: the most relentless—and dangerous—manhunter in all Texas. Where sheriffs and posses fail, he's the best man to bring in the most vicious outlaws—for a price.

→→ TABOR EVANS ←←

# LONGARM

## AND THE
## DEADLY SISTERS

J

JOVE BOOKS, NEW YORK

**THE BERKLEY PUBLISHING GROUP**
Published by the Penguin Group
Penguin Group (USA) LLC
375 Hudson Street, New York, New York 10014

USA • Canada • UK • Ireland • Australia • New Zealand • India • South Africa • China

penguin.com

A Penguin Random House Company

LONGARM AND THE DEADLY SISTERS

A Jove Book / published by arrangement with the author

Copyright © 2014 by Penguin Group (USA) LLC.
Penguin supports copyright. Copyright fuels creativity, encourages diverse voices,
promotes free speech, and creates a vibrant culture. Thank you for buying an authorized
edition of this book and for complying with copyright laws by not reproducing, scanning,
or distributing any part of it in any form without permission. You are supporting writers
and allowing Penguin to continue to publish books for every reader.

JOVE® is a registered trademark of Penguin Group (USA) LLC.
The "J" design is a trademark of Penguin Group (USA) LLC.

For information, address: The Berkley Publishing Group,
a division of Penguin Group (USA) LLC,
375 Hudson Street, New York, New York 10014.

ISBN: 978-0-515-15484-9

PUBLISHING HISTORY
Jove mass-market edition / September 2014

PRINTED IN THE UNITED STATES OF AMERICA

10  9  8  7  6  5  4  3  2  1

Cover illustration by Milo Sinovcic.

This is a work of fiction. Names, characters, places, and incidents either are the product
of the author's imagination or are used fictitiously, and any resemblance to actual persons,
living or dead, business establishments, events, or locales is entirely coincidental.

If you purchased this book without a cover, you should be aware that this book is
stolen property. It was reported as "unsold and destroyed" to the publisher, and neither
the author nor the publisher has received any payment for this "stripped book."

# Chapter 1

Deputy Marshal Custis Long turned his collar up against the driving snow as he made his way up Colfax Avenue toward the Federal Building. Denver's sidewalks had not yet been shoveled and the footing was treacherous as workers tried to get to their offices and businesses. Just up ahead of him, a stout woman bundled up in a heavy woolen coat stepped on a patch of ice and fell hard. Longarm, trying not to fall himself, hurried up to assist the woman.

"Are you hurt?" he asked with genuine concern as he knelt by her side.

"Hell yes, I'm hurt! I busted my ass."

The woman was in her fifties, red-faced from the cold, but she was smiling. "Say, handsome, you want to give this fat lady a hand?"

"Sure," Longarm replied, helping her to her feet. "Are you sure that you're all right?"

"To be perfectly honest, only my pride is injured," she

admitted. "I guess that being fat and having more padding does have a few advantages while trying to walk on this ice."

"I hope you make it to wherever you're going without another hard fall."

"Not likely, but we all have to get to work even in this horrible winter weather, don't we?"

"Sure do."

"Say, you look familiar." She turned her head first one way and then the other like a parrot. "Why, you're the one that they call Longarm! You're a famous United States marshal!"

"I am."

She gave him a good look from the top of his flat, snuff-brown hat to the toes of his overshoes, lingering for a moment on his crotch. "Well, young man, I'll bet that's not the *only* thing long about you!"

Longarm's jaw dropped and as he watched her scuttle down the icy sidewalk, he began to laugh.

Once inside the building he stomped the snow off his overshoes and hung his coat on a line of hooks provided for government employees as well as the public. Clancy O'Dell was sipping his usual cup of bracing hot coffee. The man reminded Longarm of a picture he'd seen of a walrus with his bushy mustache and big, corpulent body.

"Morning, Clancy."

"Morning, Custis," the man replied. "Real pisser of a storm, this one."

"That it is."

"I doubt that you fellas up there in the marshal's office have much to do when the weather gets this bad."

"You'd be wrong about that," Longarm replied. "Criminals are often smart enough to take advantage of bad weather."

The big guard nodded. "For a fact?"

"Yep. Even the number of train robberies increases in bad weather."

Clancy mulled that over for a minute just as Longarm was about to climb the stairs to his second floor office. "Well, that doesn't make much sense to me because they'd be leaving tracks in the snow easy enough for a lawman like you to follow."

"Good point," Longarm agreed. "But most lawmen don't like to go out in storms that can cover those tracks in a hurry."

"Oh," Clancy said, "sure, I see your point there, Marshal Long. Yes, I do."

Longarm continued up the stairs to his office. Truth be known, he hated being cooped up in the Federal Building for days waiting for some good assignment that would bring him an interesting challenge and even a little danger. And while he was a capable enough writer, he didn't like to do the damnable reports that were a requirement of his job. Mostly, when he had to be stuck in an office he brought along a book to read so that the hours would pass quickly.

"Custis!"

Longarm looked up from his desk to see his boss, Marshal Billy Vail, waving impatiently at him from the other side of the room. Longarm came to his feet, passed several other marshals, and joined Billy in the man's private office.

"I've got something right up your alley," Billy said, motioning for Longarm to take a chair. "It's a job that I wouldn't wish on anyone else but neither would I trust to anyone else."

"I'm listening." Longarm stretched his six-foot-four-inch frame out and studied Billy, instantly curious as to what the man had in mind.

"Have you ever heard of United States Senator Taft Baker?"

"The name sounds familiar."

"Well, it should because he has always been involved in railroad legislation. He was one of the ones that pushed to get funding for the transcontinental railroad."

"That was way back in '65, wasn't it?"

"About then, yeah," Billy said. "I met the man a few times when I was called back to Washington, DC, and he was one of the most flamboyant and colorful politicians I'd ever seen. He was tall, like you, and even when he got older he remained damned feisty and ready to fight at the drop of a hat. Why, when he was in his seventies, he whipped a senator from Virginia right on the steps of Congress! And the senator from Virginia was thirty years younger than Baker and said to be a big fella."

"Sounds like this Senator Baker was quite a man."

"He was. I liked him and although he was hated and feared by his opposition in Congress, everyone respected the hell out of him."

"So what has the senator to do with me?"

Billy leaned back in his chair and laced his fingers behind his bald spot. "I just learned that Senator Baker was murdered by his twin mistresses in Sacramento, California. The pair got away and word is that they have come to Denver to hide with friends or relatives."

"Whoa!" Longarm cried. "Did I hear you right? You said *twin* mistresses?"

Billy was a little prudish when it came to talking about sex and now his face turned pink with embarrassment. "It's not something that I want you to tell everyone in the office about."

"Go on."

Billy sighed. "I guess that Taft Baker was married for

quite a few years when his wife died last winter in Sacramento. There were two sisters . . . nurses . . . that had taken care of Mrs. Baker and, when she passed, they just sort of stayed on with the senator."

" 'Stayed on'?"

"That's right. At first no one thought anything about it but when the sisters never left, the rumors started flying." Billy cleared his throat. "I understand that the sisters are in their late twenties and quite attractive. It's also said that they are identical twins so you can't hardly tell them apart except perhaps if they were undressed because one has a large mole . . . well, never mind."

"No," Longarm said, very interested. "Go on! This story is getting better by the minute."

"I don't have much more to tell you," Billy said, picking up a telegram and waving it over his desk. "But apparently the senator was found shot in his bed, naked and with a big grin on his face. At the same time the sisters went missing."

"So there's no actual proof that they shot the senator?"

"You're right," Billy said. "But there was no one else living in the house with the senator when he met his demise. And the authorities have sent out information that neither of the sisters were really nurses."

"They were imposters."

"And quite possibly murderesses."

Longarm shook his head. "Well, this is an interesting case, I'll say that much. What are their names?"

"Hilda and Pearl Olsen."

"And you say they have friends and relatives here in Denver?"

"I'm not sure if that is true or not," Billy admitted. "But arresting the pair would be a real feather in our caps. It would make front-page news and help me get a raise in our budget . . . especially if they were tried in Sacramento and found guilty of murdering the senator. Custis, it would be very helpful not only to my career and yours, but to everyone in this department."

"Would that also include a long overdue raise in pay?"

"It might," Bill replied. "And it would also give us a lot of clout with Washington . . . something that we don't enjoy right now."

Longarm understood. Billy was always worried about "the budget" and if this would help get everyone in this office a nice raise . . . then that alone was a good enough incentive to try to find Senator Baker's killers.

"So," Longarm said, "what evidence do we have that these sisters might be here?"

Billy picked up a telegram. "This says that the father of the Olsen sisters might be living around here. No address but his first name is Dane."

"Any idea where I'd start looking for Dane Olsen?"

"No," Billy admitted.

Longarm frowned. "There are probably a lot of people named Olsen in Denver but I can start checking. It would help if I knew what the father does for a living."

"I'm sorry."

Longarm came to his feet. "We don't even know for certain if Dane even exists or lives in our town."

"He exists," Billy countered. "You see, Dane spent six years in a California prison for attempting to rob a stagecoach. When he was released, he left the state the very next day."

"So," Longarm mused. "The man robbed stagecoaches. Well, at least we know that he understands a thing or two about guns and horses."

"I'd say that is a fair conclusion. And perhaps stage-coaches."

"We're really working on damned little information here, Billy. Dane Olsen might have changed his name."

"I'm sorry, Custis. We don't know for sure if Dane or his daughters are here and I'm not sure that there is any evidence to prove that they murdered Senator Baker. But he was a very prominent politician and public figure, and we have to do everything we can to apprehend the sisters and get them back to Sacramento for questioning and possibly being charged with murder."

"Was Dane Olsen released from prison about the same time as the senator was murdered in his bed?"

"Good question. I'll send a telegram back to Sacramento and find out."

"Do it right away," Longarm said, "because it's possible that the sisters were *not* the ones that murdered Senator Baker but instead it was their father."

"It's a mess," Billy admitted. "I know I'm giving you more questions than answers but—"

"I got it," Longarm interrupted. "Do we even have descriptions on what the sisters look like?"

Billy's eyes jumped back to the telegram. "It just says that they both had long, blonde hair and blue eyes. Oh, and tall. Both stand nearly six feet."

"They are probably Scandinavian. Anything else?"

"Nothing other than they are tall and very attractive and identical."

"Well," Longarm said, standing up. "Two tall, identically blonde, and beautiful young women won't go unnoticed for long even in a town this size. I'll start asking around."

"Ask around a lot, Custis. This is *really* important."

"I will," Longarm promised. "But this thing about Dane is also a worry. If he was released from prison shortly before the senator's murder and immediately left California, then that tells me that he might very well be involved along with Hilda and Pearl. Was anything missing from the senator's home after he was found dead?"

"Yes. He had a safe in his office hidden behind a portrait of President Lincoln. The portrait was moved and the safe was open. No one has any idea how much money or other valuables were in the safe, but the senator was a wealthy man. In addition, there were a few other items that were missing."

"Such as?"

"A gold pocket watch and chain. It was made in France and was very valuable. There were also several pieces of art that were removed and taken."

"Maybe it was a robbery that had nothing to do with any of the Olsen people."

Billy shrugged. "No one will ever know until they are arrested and brought back to California for questioning. However, that does seem unlikely."

"And why is that?"

"If the sisters or their father are innocent, why would they just up and vanish right after Senator Baker was shot to death in his bed?"

"Good question," Longarm had to admit.

"Custis, if you need help I can—"

"Let me do some scouting around and make a few inquiries on my own first," Longarm interrupted.

"I don't know where to even tell you to begin searching."

"I'll give it some thought as soon as I've poured a cup of coffee," Longarm told the man. "And anyway, I'd sure rather be outside moving around and talking to people than sitting at my desk watching snow pelt the windows."

"Yes, I'm sure you would." Billy paused. "You know, if you'd like to one day be promoted, then you'll have to get comfortable with more desk time."

"I don't want to be promoted," Longarm said. "You're good at what you do and I'm good at what I do, so why should anything change?"

"A promotion would bring you a significant raise in your salary."

"And ulcers." Longarm headed out the door.

# Chapter 2

Longarm had no idea where he might start to look for the Olsen sisters or if they were even in these parts. But he knew a lot of people in Denver and figured that, if he asked enough questions, he'd get some answers. Outside, the wind and snow were blowing just as hard as when he'd entered the building and so Longarm turned up his collar, screwed down his hat, and headed up Colfax Avenue. His first stop was at the newspaper office. The editor was a longtime friend named Stuart Appleton and he'd been in charge of the paper for at least the past ten years so he knew almost everyone that either accomplished something newsworthy, ran afoul of the law, or was involved in civic affairs.

"Dane Olsen won't be civic-minded," Longarm said after meeting the editor and settling into a chair. "In fact, quite the opposite."

"Has he committed a criminal act?" the tall, lanky editor asked.

"I'm not sure, but probably not in Denver."

"I do know some people named Olsen. None, however, with the first name of Dane. How old a man would he be?"

"He has two daughters in their twenties so he has to be at least in his late forties or more likely fifties."

"Do the daughters live here in Denver?"

"They may have recently arrived from California."

The editor tried to bury a smile. "You seem to be working on a lot of 'maybe this or maybe that' possibilities. Are you sure of *anything*?"

"Yes, but not something I can tell you about."

"A story?"

"Perhaps," Longarm said, knowing that nothing would entice the man into helping him more than the promise of an important future story having to do with the murder and scandal revolving around a famous senator.

"And you would immediately come to me with that story as soon as you or your superiors felt comfortable with offering that information?"

"Of course."

"All right," Appleton said, "we have an agreement."

"I suppose that we do."

The editor steepled his fingers. "Do you know what Dane Olsen does for a living?"

"I'm afraid not. He was recently released from a California prison for attempting to rob a stagecoach."

"Do you think that he's tried to rob a stagecoach here in Colorado?"

"I don't know. Maybe he did at one time. But there are not many stagecoach robberies anymore. They seem to have moved to banks and railroads in the past ten years."

"Yes."

"A man bold enough to attempt to rob a stage . . . be it

here or in California . . . is likely to have attempted to do other criminal acts," Longarm suggested. "Wouldn't you agree?"

"I would. But if this man is in his late forties or early fifties, he might . . ."

"Like I told you, Stuart, he just got out of prison after being convicted of a serious crime."

Stuart Appleton thought for a moment. "The editor who worked here before I took this job was quite an organized individual. He maintained years of records . . . little card files actually . . . of every criminal act that was of significance. It is quite possible that this person you seek did rob a stagecoach before I became editor, and if he were caught, arrested, convicted, and sentenced, he could be in those files . . . unless, of course, he's changed his name."

"How far back do the file cards go?"

"Twenty years at least. I'll be honest with you, Marshal Long, it will be a tedious, time-consuming job. It might take a couple of days to go through them."

Longarm didn't find the idea of going through the card file even a little appealing, but when you had nothing to go on you had to start by grasping at straws.

"Would you allow me to take the files?"

Appleton thought about it for a few minutes. "The card files are just notes from courtrooms and observations. There is nothing in them that is prejudicial or incriminating. However, it's not something that I'm too comfortable with giving to you."

"How about this," Longarm suggested after noting the editor's professional concern. "You have someone run the card files over to the Federal Building and give them to my boss, Marshal Billy Vail."

"I know the man. Fine gentleman."

"He is," Longarm agreed. "Marshal Vail can have an officer go through those files one by one looking for stagecoach robberies and the name of Dane Olsen."

"And I assume that this would be kept confidential . . . within house so to speak."

"It would. You have my word on it."

"I'm comfortable with that."

"Thank you, Stuart."

"You can best thank me by giving me an idea of what this is all about. You said something about two young women."

"I suppose I did."

"But you're not prepared to tell me what they might have to do with their father."

"Not yet."

"Very well. Just keep me posted. Like you, I'm a professional and I would never jeopardize your case with a premature newspaper story."

"I know that."

"I'll have the files sent over to Marshal Vail right away." Appleton started to turn back to his paperwork, but then seemed to have a thought. "Oh, perhaps this is of no value to you but there is a family named Olsen who lives just to the east of town that has a dark reputation."

"Go on."

"I briefly met the patriarch of the family many years ago. He was being sued by a competitor whom he then assaulted."

"What was the man's first name?"

"I can't begin to remember, but it's in the card file."

"*You* also keep a card file?"

Stuart Appleton shrugged. "I promised my predecessor

that I would, but I haven't done nearly as thorough a job. Hold on a moment."

Longarm stood and waited about five minutes in the editor's office until Stuart burst back into the room waving a file card. "Yes, here it is!" he proudly proclaimed. "It resulted in a hefty fine, a ten-day jail sentence, and probation."

Longarm took the card and read it. "The patriarch's name is Dane Olsen. Do you know where the Olsen place is located east of town?"

"Afraid not." The editor scowled. "But you might ask the local sheriff or even one of the stables here in town."

"I understand your suggestion that I go to see the sheriff . . . I'd planned to do so anyway. But why would you suggest I visit Denver's stables in search of information?"

"One of the Olsen men used to own a livery and have a stagecoach business that ran between Denver and Cheyenne before they built the railroad and put him out of business."

"I see."

"Be careful," the editor warned. "I seem to recall that it was a large and violent clan."

"Thanks for the warning and the information."

"Might not have any connection at all," Appleton conceded. "Maybe not worth going out in this bad weather."

"I'll wait until the storm passes."

Appleton chuckled. "You've left a lot of gaps in the story, but from what I'm reading between the lines . . . I'd say *your* storm is just beginning."

Longarm didn't have a response, so he headed for the sheriff's office, hoping the man might have some further information on Dane Olsen.

# Chapter 3

Longarm went to the sheriff's office where he knew everyone and received a warm greeting. Sheriff Patterson was a veteran lawman with plenty of knowledge of Denver, its politics, and its problem makers.

"Well, well," Patterson said, grinning as he stuck out his hand, "if it isn't the famous Longarm come to visit us poor peons that risk our lives in poverty and obscurity."

"Cut the crap," Longarm said good-naturedly. "How have you been since I was here last?"

"Older and poorer," the sheriff said without rancor. "But it's a job that has to be done so here I am. Are you still tomcatting around every night?"

"No," Longarm answered. "I manage to get a good night's sleep most of the time."

"Don't go and soil your reputation as a lady killer," Patterson advised. "You're still a relatively young man, although your years of hard loving and fighting are starting to show."

"Sheriff, I can always count on you to ruin my day."

"Coffee?"

"Nope," Longarm answered. "The last cup I drank here was stronger than horse piss and it gave me the shits."

Patterson roared with laughter. "Sit down, Custis. I'd like to think you just dropped by to say hello to an old friend but I know you better. What is it you want this time?"

"Some information."

"About who or what?" the sheriff asked, motioning Longarm to a three-legged chair.

"I am looking for Olsens," Longarm said. "Two sisters, tall, blonde, and beautiful, might have murdered a United States senator named—"

"Taft Baker," Patterson interrupted. "Yeah, I read about that in the Sacramento paper."

"And how would you get one of those?"

"I'm planning to retire in a year or two and move to California where the weather is easier on my health," Patterson confessed. "My wife is all for it and we've just had enough of this bitter Denver winter weather. So I subscribe to the *Sacramento Bee* and get it once a week. The murder of the senator was all over the front page a few weeks ago."

"Do you still have the paper?" Longarm asked. "If you do, then I'd sure like to read it."

"I do have it, but I want it back when you're finished. There are some ads in the paper for houses that I'm keeping track of."

"Then you really are serious about moving."

"As serious as a whore at a revival meeting." Patterson chuckled at his own joke, and then said, "You didn't come here to look at a newspaper. What are you really after?"

"Just some information on the Olsen family."

"Which one?"

"The one that has a place east of town and is owned by a man named Dane Olsen."

Sheriff Patterson smiled and actually clapped his hands in glee. "Dane is rotten to the core. His father, Daniel Olsen, was meaner than a rattlesnake, but he's dead and most everyone said good riddance."

"How'd he die?"

"Old Daniel got stinking, dirty drunk, fell off a heavily laden buckboard, and the back wheel of his wagon rolled over his throat. I hear that it was a very hard death with him choking and gurgling, trying to cuss. The wheel almost cut his head off and while that sounds gruesome, it was a just reward for a lawless and vicious life."

"How long ago did this happen?"

"Maybe a month ago. I heard that his funeral was very well attended because so many hated his guts. They tried to bury Daniel here at the Forever Pines Cemetery, but the director refused to take him so he was buried on his own miserable little ranch."

"Did you know of his son, Dane?"

"Sure." Patterson took a sip of his very bad and strong coffee. "Dane went to California to see his daughters, Hilda and Pearl. He must have run out of money because he tried to rob a stage that ran up to Placerville, but he was shot and wounded. Did a spell in prison."

"If you read the Sacramento paper every week you probably learned that he was released."

Patterson nodded. "Are you about to suggest that Dane Olsen and his girls had something to do with the murder of Senator Baker?"

"It's a real possibility. Pearl and Hilda worked for the senator as nurses and . . ."

"Nurses! Ha! The only thing they could nurse is a man's sexual organs and I suspect Pearl would be real good at that."

"And not Hilda?"

The sheriff frowned. "I haven't seen the girls for years and years. But I have heard stories of them and how they were doing in California."

"Tell me about that."

"Pearl took the low road and from what I heard, she did real well as a prostitute in San Francisco. Hilda was different. She became a pretty skilled piano player and singer. She worked saloons, but I'm told she wasn't a high-priced whore like Pearl. I had heard that they were working for Senator Baker at the time of his death, but I couldn't believe it."

"Well, you can now." Longarm shifted his balance on the three-legged chair. "Is this office so poor it can't afford a better chair than this?" he complained.

"I like it because it keeps my visitors a little off balance."

Longarm stood up and pushed the broken chair over. "I don't. But tell anything more that you can about those sisters and their father."

"Dane," Patterson began, "was the apple that didn't fall far from the tree. He was of the same cut of cloth as his father, big, violent, and always looking for a fight or a chance to make quick, easy money. I had some run-ins with him and he was dangerous. I pistol-whipped him so hard one time that I was sure I'd killed him, but he recovered and was just as mean and cocky as ever."

"Have you heard anything about Dane or his girls returning to the homestead?"

"Nope and I hope they didn't."

"I'm going to find out as soon as this weather clears. I'll rent a horse and go pay them a visit, but I need some directions."

"Custis, you don't need directions. You need sound advice and I'm going to give it to you right now. Dane is bad to the bone and he has several sons that are trying to outdo him in that regard."

"How many men might be out there at the Olsen ranch?"

"Four, including Dane if he's come back, and I sure as hell hope he hasn't. Tell you what," Patterson said. "If you are going to wait for better weather, then I'll ride out with you."

"I can handle it myself."

"I'm sure you can! But you see, if there are at least the two of us, then you might not have to pull your gun and fight for your life. That makes sense, doesn't it?"

"Yeah, it does."

"Then it's settled," the Denver sheriff said. "As soon as the weather clears we'll ride out and pay those bastards a visit."

"My boss wants me to arrest Hilda and Pearl and see that they are taken back to Sacramento for questioning."

"Hmm," the lawman mused, "if they are there, that won't go over too well with the Olsen clan."

"I don't care about hurting their feelings," Longarm said bluntly. "All I care about is doing my job and getting the sisters to California where the authorities there are eager to question them. If they're innocent of Senator Baker's death, then they ought to at least have some information on who might have killed the famous legislator. If they're guilty, they need to be brought to trial, sentenced, and suffer their due punishment."

"I couldn't agree more," Patterson said. "And to tell you the truth, if Dane has returned, then I want to know about it before he comes into town."

"How long do you think this storm might last?" Longarm asked, more to himself than to the lawman.

"Who knows? But I'm hoping we'll have clear weather tomorrow."

"I hope so," Longarm said. "I'm not a man who likes to wait around."

"I know. I know. I've seen you enough to know that when you have a hunt started, you get as nervous as a long-tailed cat under a rocking chair."

Longarm barked a laugh. "I'll be back at the first sign of blue skies and we'll rent a couple of horses."

"Make sure that you have your gun loaded and a rifle ready to use just in case."

"In case the clan opens fire on us?"

"That's right. I expect the Olsen clan would like nothing better than to shoot us out of our saddles and feed our bodies to their hogs."

"They have a hog farm?"

"And a still where they brew rotgut whiskey." Patterson came to his feet and stretched. He was not a big man, but he was solid muscle. "I sure would like to catch sight of those two Olsen women that you intend to arrest."

"When did they leave Denver?"

"Many years ago. Their mother ran away with them to California and I expect that she thought she might find gold in the Sierras or in the pockets of miners. I heard they went broke, lived up in Virginia City on the Comstock Lode, but then returned to California because the old woman was starting to get bad rheumatism. She was a looker in her day, I'll tell you."

"And so apparently are her twin daughters."

"Not surprising. Good thing they didn't get their father's looks. I never did understand why that woman married him."

"Maybe he forced her into the marriage."

"Maybe."

"It's happened before," Longarm offered.

"Well, I'm just glad that Victoria ran off with the girls and I heard she lived a decent life and is buried in Sacramento."

Longarm said nothing. But he could see real emotion and sadness on Sheriff Patterson's rugged face and wondered if the lawman might actually have been in love with Mrs. Victoria Olsen.

# Chapter 4

"Marshal Long?"

Custis turned to see a pretty woman hurrying to catch up with him, but just as she drew near, she slipped on the ice and fell hard.

"Lola?" he asked, rushing over to help her but catching a patch of ice and landing heavily beside her. He winced and managed to ask, "Are you all right?"

Miss Lola Zahn made a face. "I'm not so sure. How are you?"

"I really landed hard. Damned ice! Let's see if we can get up and get out of this blowing snow."

He helped her to her feet and they were both limping as they rounded a corner to get out of the worst of the wind and stand close to an old brick building.

"Not a very nice way to meet again," Lola said, managing a smile.

"No, it wasn't."

"I'm just visiting my parents for a few days," she told

him. "They're getting up in years and since moving to Cheyenne I don't get to see them very often. But I wish I'd have waited until after the storm."

"Are you hurt?"

"I'm not sure," she admitted, placing a gloved hand on her shapely hip. "I think I might have really bruised my bottom."

"Now that would be a shame," he said, well remembering that curvaceous turn of her buttocks and much more. "My apartment is close. We could go there and check ourselves out . . . you know, make sure that there's no serious damage."

She had rosy cheeks and blue eyes. Lola was all bundled up but even a heavy coat couldn't hide the fact that she was large breasted.

"You're looking at me like a wolf might a lamb," she teased. "I'm not sure that I should go up to your apartment. I remember what would always happen."

"And we loved it," he reminded her. "Come on up."

"Don't you have a job anymore?"

"Sure, but I'm doing an investigation and kind of stalled until this weather clears. What about you?"

"I told my parents that I'd be back to join them for dinner this evening."

"No boyfriends or husband yet?"

"No. Well, there are a few eligible bachelors that have been taking me to dinner up in Cheyenne, but not one that has truly caught my fancy. The truth is, I see a lot of young women my age who are married and already look old and tired. Then I ask myself, 'do I want to get married and have a bunch of screaming kids?' Well, I usually admit that I don't and then I tell my suitors to go find another love."

"You always were a heartbreaker."

"Not yours, that's for sure."

"Are you still painting and decorating?"

"Yes, I've gotten into sculpturing and there are quite a few rich ranching families that have given me assignments decorating their elaborate homes. I'm doing all right, Custis, and you?"

He shrugged. "About the same. I was in Arizona and Nevada last month tracking down a murderer."

"And I bet you killed rather than captured him."

"How'd you guess?"

"You always told me that if a murderer drew his gun or showed any sign of wanting to do so, you shot them on the spot. I admired that, Custis. Why should we, the taxpayers support some bloody bastard for years in a prison?"

"Lola, it's freezing out here. Why don't we go up to my apartment and I'll pour us something strong and we can catch up on old times."

"If I do, will you tell me what you're working on right now because I always found that fascinating?"

"Sure," he said, knowing he would have promised anything to get Lola Zahn up to his warm apartment and into his soft bed. "I'll fill you in."

"I'll just bet you will," she said, taking his arm as they both limped up the sidewalk.

An hour later Longarm was lying on his back with Lola bouncing vigorously up and down on his rod. He'd already taken her once in a rush and now she was having her way with his long, scarred body. His hands were on her narrow hips and he was smiling as he watched her hair bounce wildly and her mouth formed a big oval as she neared her orgasm.

"Oh, gawd!" she cried, leaning forward so that he could suck on her large breasts. "Why don't you move to Cheyenne so we can do this more often!"

"Because my job is here in Denver."

Lola began to slam her lovely but bruised bottom up and down faster and faster until she froze for an instant, let out a howl, and then collapsed in his arms, quivering like a leaf in the wind.

"Custis," she panted, turning her lovely face to look closely at him. "I've missed this."

He kissed her mouth and rolled her to the side as he looked out the window. "Still snowing and we've got a couple of hours before dark. I'll be ready to nail you at least once more before you have to leave."

"You always were an insatiable beast," she said, kissing his lips. "You've the morals of an alley cat but the body of an Adonis."

"I'd say the same except that you're a Venus. Lola, why don't you move back here to Denver? We could start up again and I'm sure that your parents would be overjoyed and very grateful."

"In truth, my mother drives me crazy. She's always fretting about this or that. Right now she's afraid that the snow will get so heavy on her roof that it will cave in. And she worries about money all the time even though she and my father are well fixed."

"If you returned to live here, you wouldn't have to live with them."

"Are you saying that I could live here with you and we could screw ourselves silly every day until I got pregnant and you decided you wanted no part of fatherhood and I hated being fat and sick?"

"Hmm," he mused. "Do you really think it would happen that way between us?"

"If we screwed every day I guarantee that I'd soon be with child and you'd soon be regretting that I ever returned from Cheyenne."

"That's probably right. But . . ."

"I know. We love doing this to and for each other. But you're a womanizer and I'm . . . well, I think I'd make a lousy wife and mother. Maybe in five or ten years we can talk this over again, but for now I'd just as soon you tell me about the case you're working on after you pour us another couple shots of your good whiskey."

"I'll do that, lovely lady."

Lola laughed. "You know I'm no lady! I don't know why you'd say a thing like that."

"Me, neither," he admitted, "because you're a wanton woman."

"Now that's being honest." She waited until he'd brought her another shot of whiskey, then she sat up in his bed, crossed her legs, and said, "Okay, tell me all about what you're up to and don't you dare leave a thing out of the story."

For the next half hour, he told her about his case and how Sheriff Patterson had agreed to join him after the weather cleared and ride out to the Olsen ranch.

"Sounds pretty dangerous to me," Lola fretted. "Is the sheriff a capable man?"

"Very capable. He shoots fast and he shoots straight, but I'm hoping it doesn't come to that. Patterson isn't going to push things too far and my intention is to get some information."

"What if Dane or his daughters aren't at the ranch?"

"Then I'll be asking where they can be found."

"What if they refuse to answer?" Lola persisted. "I mean, why would they tell you and Sheriff Patterson anything?"

"I don't know," Longarm admitted, "but it's a starting point. I really don't have much else to work with right now."

"I wonder if Hilda and Pearl really murdered and robbed that senator . . . or if it was their father."

"So do I." Longarm took a sip of whiskey. "So why don't you forget about having dinner tonight with your parents and have dinner with me? I'll take you to a nice steakhouse and we can come back here and have another romp."

Lola Zahn laughed heartily. "Well, my ass is bruised purple from the fall and it hurts. You want to pole me two or three times before tomorrow morning. Can you imagine how I'd move walking out of here?"

Longarm snorted and chuckled. "I see your point. All right, dinner another night and I'll escort you home before dark."

"Like a gentleman," she said as her pretty face suddenly turned serious. "Please be careful when you and Sheriff Patterson ride out to the Olsens' ranch. They sound like very dangerous people."

"We'll be prepared," Longarm said. "In my closet I have a loaded shotgun and I'm going to take it with me when we go out there."

"I can't wait to hear if you find those tall, blonde, and twin sisters then arrest them."

"Neither can I."

"I wonder if they've got bigger jugs than these?" Lola cupped her breasts one by one. "Or ones that stand up nice and tall."

Longarm almost choked on his whiskey. "You always did have a way of shocking me with what comes out of your mouth."

"I enjoy doing that," she admitted. "Because I imagine you've heard almost everything there is to hear from women. So if I can throw you something unexpected and get a real reaction, I'm pleased."

Longarm nodded with understanding. "I've missed you, Lola. And not just because I lust for your body. I miss the laughter we shared and the way we used to talk about things."

"I'll talk about almost anything with you, Custis." She emptied her glass. "The truth of it is that I always thought that we are very much alike even though I'm an artist and you're a lawman."

"Strange bedfellows make for a good match."

Lola set her glass down on his bedside table. "It's starting to get dark out there. I think I should get dressed and you should walk me home before it is dark and we can't see the ice on the sidewalks."

"We could see the ice earlier and that didn't keep us both from falling hard."

"I know."

"We should have a go at each other one more time," he said, almost embarrassed by how easily she could arouse him without even trying.

"A quickie, then," she said agreeably.

"I'll take whatever I can get," he said, placing his own glass down and gently pushing apart her lovely thighs.

# Chapter 5

"Well," Longarm said as he entered the office and stomped the snow off his boots, "the storm has passed and I thought that it's about time that we took that ride out to talk to the Olsen clan. Maybe even find the twin sisters."

"I'm not eager to see the men," Patterson said, putting wood into his potbellied stove, "and it's going to be a damn cold ride out there."

"Sheriff, I'm going out there alone if I have to."

"No," Patterson replied, "I'll go with you because I think they'd shoot you out of the saddle before you could get close enough to have a conversation."

"Thanks for your help."

"Don't mention it. If Dane is back, that's something I need to know. And I sure would like to see his tall, good-looking twin daughters."

"You're starting to drool."

The Denver sheriff barked a self-depreciating laugh and reached for his coat and hat. "All right. Let's go over to the

Acme Stable and rent saddle horses. He walked over to his rifle rack and selected, then loaded a Winchester repeater. "You well armed?"

Longarm reached under his heavy coat to show the man that he had a double-barreled and sawed-off shotgun. "I'm prepared for the worst."

"Good!" Patterson nodded with approval. "Let's ride. The sooner we get started the sooner we get back to this stove."

"Your fire will be dead by the time we return."

"Let's just hope *we* don't wind up dead."

Longarm couldn't think of an appropriate reply so he just opened the door and they filed out into a clear, bitterly cold morning.

An hour later they were trotting along the snowy road headed for the Olsen ranch, trying to keep warm. Their horses were frisky and fractious in the cold weather and the Rocky Mountains looming to the west were heavily blanketed. Looking up at them Patterson said, "I'll bet the snow up there in Central City and Leadville is forty feet deep."

"At least," Longarm agreed. "I don't know how they put up with winters that high."

"They stay drunk," Patterson explained. "Or head for the low country. That's what I used to do when I was young and full of piss and vinegar. I was a miner."

"I didn't know that."

"Well, I was . . . for about a year and then I saw a couple of men that I worked with being carried out on stretchers deader than lead. The shaft they were working in had collapsed and it took two days to reach the bodies. Wasn't much left of them to bury and everyone agreed that they should have just closed down the shaft and left them there forever."

"A lot of men die in those mines."

"They sure do," Patterson agreed. "More than die from bullets and that's when I began to buy more ammunition than whiskey and start practicing with my draw and shooting aim. When I figured that I was better than ninety-five percent of the crowd with a six-gun, I applied for a job in Leadville as a deputy. Two days later the marshal I worked for was shot in the back and since I was the only deputy, the job fell on me."

"Did you ever catch the sheriff's ambusher and bring him to justice?" Longarm asked.

"Sure did! I gave him lead poisoning, which was his due justice. I worked a lot of those wild mining towns before I got smart and came to Denver. I worked my way up here mostly because the former sheriffs were shot to death, scared off, or beaten out of their senses. I've been around longer than any of them, but sometimes I still wonder why I'm wearing a badge."

"You said you were retiring to Sacramento next year."

"I may retire sooner than that. Agnes, my wife, is ready to go anytime and we've managed to build up a good savings account. Agnes cooks and cleans and every penny she makes goes into the bank. We live off my salary and it is lean, but we make do. No, sir, I may not wait even until the snow melts to pack up with Agnes and head for sunny California."

"I hope you and Agnes like it there and live long and well."

The sheriff glanced sideways at Longarm. "Right now I'm just prayin' we both don't get shot out of our saddles."

"Cheer up," Longarm said. "With these heavy coats on, our collars turned up, and our hats pulled low over our faces, they won't even recognize you until we are among them. At that point, we'll have the edge."

"You make damn good and sure that your sawed-off shotgun is ready to roar. Agnes would never forgive you if I get killed today."

"I'll do my best," Longarm vowed as he began to wish that he'd come out to confront the Olsen family all by himself.

The Olsen homestead was off by itself in the lee of a hillside. As they approached Longarm could see that the original house had been a soddie, cut into the side of the hill. But over the years, just as many people on the high plains had done, the soddie had become a storage place and had been replaced by a more permanent house with a few barns and corrals. There were no trees, but plenty of old wagons and stagecoaches rotting in the weather. Six horses, a slew of ugly pigs in a big, muddy pen, several skinny chickens, and a few dogs completed the picture, which was one of a hard-scrabble existence.

The ranch dogs saw Longarm and Sheriff Patterson when they were still a half mile away. The dogs set up a racket, and by the time that Longarm and the sheriff rode into the junkyard littered with broken wagons four armed men and two old women were standing on the porch . . . and the old women held rifles.

"This doesn't look too friendly," Longarm said. "Which one is Dane?"

Patterson squinted into the glare of snow and sunlight. "Gray-bearded fella wearing the black derby hat. He's the one to watch closest, but I sure don't see the twin sisters."

"They could be hiding inside," Longarm offered. "Or they could be in one of the barns or behind a broken-down stagecoach with rifles. You need to be ready for anything and everything, Sheriff. I don't want you to tell them that I'm a federal officer. Just strike up a friendly conversation."

"About what?"

"About whatever you can think of. Say that we're here because someone claimed that the Olsens had stolen a horse or mule. Get them talking and I'll see if I can move around a bit."

"They won't allow us to search the house or the barns."

"No hospitality, huh?"

"They only thing these people will give you is lead poisoning."

"I need to get them in range of the scattergun under my coat," Longarm said. "If they pull weapons on us, I'd prefer not to kill the women."

Sheriff Patterson nodded, his face pale and solemn. "It would set hard on my soul to have to shoot the Olsen women."

"Mine, too," Longarm added, "but those old crones look to me like they would kill us both without so much as a passing regret."

"You got that pegged right," Patterson said in a low voice. "If they get the drop on us, we're going to be feeding their hogs long before sundown."

Longarm shook off that unpleasant image and wrapped his reins around his saddle horse so that when he stopped in the ranch yard, he would have the use of both hands. Seeing him do that, Sheriff Patterson was not too proud to do the same.

# Chapter 6

"That's close enough, Sheriff!" Dane Olsen shouted from his porch. "State your damned business and keep your hands up where we can see 'em."

Longarm muttered under his breath. "So much for the getting the drop on 'em or having any hope of getting into the house."

"I knew we wouldn't," Sheriff Patterson said. "I'd advise you to do what they say."

Longarm placed both of his hands on the saddle horn and forced a frozen smile. "Afternoon," he called, expecting no response.

"What do you want?" Dane demanded, as his sons and two old women stared hard at them.

"We're just riding out to check on folks and make sure that they're not frozen or starving after this storm." Patterson gulped and tried to sound as if he were actually concerned with their welfare. "How are you folks doing today?"

"We're fine as you can plainly see," one of the brothers growled.

"That's good to hear."

"Who's that big fella with you, Patterson?"

Longarm knew it was his turn to speak and so he said, "I'm Custis Long."

"You look familiar," Dane drawled, squinting hard. "Have I seen you before?"

"I don't think so."

"No matter. Right now I want to see the ass ends of your horses."

It seemed clear that Sheriff Patterson was about to rein his horse around so Longarm said, "I'm looking for Hilda and Pearl."

One of the women raised her shotgun toward him. "What business you got with them girls!"

Longarm took a deep breath. "They were in Sacramento helping a very famous man, Senator Baker, who died. The senator has left them money in his will but they need to come into town and sign some papers."

"How *much* money!" the other older woman demanded.

"Be a little more than a thousand dollars for each of them . . . but if they can't place their rightful claim for the inheritance, it will go to a very fine charity in Sacramento run by the Beloved Sisters of Charity."

"Screw them holier-than-thou Sisters of Charity!" the woman shouted, spitting a stream of tobacco into the yard. "Who are you!"

"A magistrate," Longarm admitted.

"A what?"

"A servant of the court."

"You came all the way from Sacramento to tell us that

Hilda and Pearl are gettin' a thousand dollars from that famous senator they worked for?" Dane asked, clearly skeptical.

"Senator Taft Baker was very fond of Hilda and Pearl."

"I'll just bet the old bastard was," a tall, raggedly dressed man in his late teens hissed. "But what if we don't believe you?"

"Then we'll ride off and the Beloved Sisters of Charity will not only thank you folks, but they will offer up prayers in your behalf," Longarm said, struggling to maintain his frozen smile. "I'd say that's a real act of Christian charity on your family's part."

"Now wait a damned minute here," Dane countered. "We ain't sayin' that we're willin' to give any thousand dollars to some shittin' Sacramento charity!"

"Two thousand," Sheriff Patterson corrected. "One thousand for *each* of the sisters."

"And a little extra," Longarm added.

The Olsen clan exchanged glances with each other, clearly not sure of what to say or do. Finally, Dane said, "How about one of us sign for Hilda and Pearl?"

"That won't do," Patterson answered. "The twins have to sign in front of a witness and our highest Denver judge."

"Damn," Dane swore.

"Sounds fishy to me," the tallest of the old women said. "Don't seem likely that someone would come all the way out here from California to tell us about that money those girls earned doin' the dirties."

"She's right," Dane said, spitting a stream of tobacco. "Don't make much sense."

Longarm had anticipated the question and had a ready answer. "It does when you understand that the senator and the most honorable Judge Fable were lifelong friends."

"Honorable Judge Fable?" Dane said, looking confused.

"That's right," Patterson said. "And a better judge you'll never find anywhere on this Earth."

"None of us think too kindly toward judges," Dane hissed. "Hilda and Pearl ain't here and if the money is to go to them, then we'll sure as hell see that they git it."

"Well, Dane," Patterson said after a few moments of deliberation, "we'll be on our way. But if you hear from your daughters, tell them that they have until Monday afternoon at five o'clock to come in and make their claims for their rightful inheritances."

"Nice meeting you," Longarm said, reining his horse around and hoping the clan didn't open fire as they rode away.

"Wait a damned minute!" the Dane shouted. "What day is *this*?"

"Saturday."

"Then they have just *two* days?"

"That's right!" Longarm called over his shoulder, smiling because now it was clear that the clan was either hiding Hilda and Pearl at this run-down homestead or knew where the young women were to be found.

"Judge *Fable*?" Patterson asked when they were out of hearing range.

Longarm relaxed. "That's right."

Patterson shook his head. "You were taking a big chance that at least one of them knew what the word 'fable' meant."

Longarm twisted around in his saddle to see the dirty and ragged clan arguing. "Not really."

# Chapter 7

Longarm sat down across from Billy Vail and kicked his boots up on the man's desk. "So that's where we stand right now," he said. "I've no doubt in my mind that Dane Olsen and his twin daughters will ride into town and try to collect that money."

"They'll probably bring the entire clan and there could be a lot of trouble when you arrest Hilda and Pearl."

Longarm frowned. "I've been thinking about that and you are right. Sheriff Patterson is talking about retirement and I don't want to bring any grief down on him or his wife."

"Maybe you should take up residence at his office," Billy suggested. "And I could supply you with a couple of men as backups."

"Let me give it some thought," Longarm replied.

Billy studied him. "I can't believe you said that this was being hired by a 'Judge Fable.'"

Longarm shrugged his broad shoulders and headed out the door.

On Monday morning Longarm returned to the office and said to Billy, "I decided to take up your offer of some backup. I'm sure that Sheriff Patterson and I can handle the Olsen men, but if we have some extra guns then maybe it will prevent a shootout."

"Good thinking," Billy said, looking pleased. "You sound like you're pretty certain they'll appear today."

"They're hardscrabble and hungry," Longarm answered. "Even their hogs are skinny and mean-looking. The women look old, but they're probably still middle-aged."

"I can give you deputies Jasper White and Larry Pence," Billy offered.

"Not Larry," Longarm said. "He's too unpredictable and we don't like each other much."

"Oh?"

"Larry has a big chip on his shoulder because of a woman we both admired."

"You took a woman away from him?"

"I didn't take anything away," Longarm said. "The woman just wasn't interested in Larry, but she felt differently about me. She did what she wanted to do and I had no part of it."

"I wouldn't go that far," Billy said. "Who else would you want besides Jasper?"

"Clyde Peterson," Longarm said. "He's steady and he will take orders."

"All right then," Billy said. "I'll bring them into the office and you can tell them how you want this handled . . . providing I approve."

"Sure," Longarm said. "The way I see it, all Jasper and Clyde need to do is appear at the moment we take Pearl and Hilda into custody. If there's going to be trouble, that's when it will start."

# Chapter 8

"Damn," Longarm swore as he and the two federal deputy marshals walked swiftly up Colfax Avenue at a little before eight o'clock the next morning, "unless I'm mistaken, that's Dane Olsen and his family arriving at the sheriff's office!"

"What the hell are we going to do now?" Clyde asked.

"I'll go on up ahead and intercept Dane and his sons. You and Jasper move away but keep your eyes on that buggy with the three women."

"You think two of them are the twin sisters, Hilda and Pearl?"

"Have to be," Longarm said. "And the third one is probably that old crone that I saw standing on the front porch of the Olsen cabin with a shotgun. Don't take your eyes off any of them for a minute."

"We'll be ready for whatever happens," Jasper promised as the two men distanced themselves from Longarm.

Longarm didn't want to run, but he walked up the street

as fast as he could, arriving at the sheriff's door just as Dane and his two surly-looking sons were about to enter.

"Good morning, Dane," Longarm said, pushing between the man and the door. "You and the family must have left bright and early this morning to get here so soon."

"We're homesteaders," the man snapped. "We get up with the chickens and go to bed with the chickens. We ain't got no easy job like you and the marshal suckin' off the teat of the poor public."

Longarm bit back a smart retort and managed to keep a smile on his face. "And you brought your daughters, I see."

"You said they had to come to get the money so where is this Judge Fable and that cash? We ain't here to talk."

"Well," Longarm said, glancing at the buggy and then noting that his fellow deputies were close by and ready for whatever trouble might take place, "first we need to get Hilda and Pearl inside where the sheriff will ask them a few questions in an attempt to establish their true identities."

"What the hell are you talking about!" Dane swore. "You think they got our cows' brands on their asses? What is this 'identity' bullshit you're talking about! They're my beauties and we're here for the money."

"I understand that," Longarm said, watching the face of the older son turn dark with anger. "But we need to have your twins step inside and answer some questions. Just a necessary formality."

"Gawdamn, Pa, I told you this was gonna be a pile of stinkin' hog shit! I don't even believe this big son of a bitch and you shouldn't, either."

Longarm turned his attention to the tall, skinny young man. "What's your name?" he asked quietly.

The kid glanced at his father, then defiantly back at Longarm. "What's it any of your business?"

Longarm's voice dropped to almost a whisper. "Son," he said quietly, "you are in serious need of an ass kicking and some proper manners."

Dane took an audible breath as everyone tensed. "Sam, maybe you and Ollie ought to go stand by the buggy with your aunt Edna while me and the girls go inside and do what needs to be done so we can get our money and get the hell out of here."

For a moment, Sam just stood there trembling, and although Longarm couldn't see the kid's right hand, he knew it was hovering close to a gun on his hip. "Sam, your father just told you to get on over to the buggy and I think that would be the healthiest thing you could do right now."

"Don't you threaten my boy!" Dane hissed.

"He's obviously too stupid to take a serious threat," Longarm told the man. "But you might just be smart enough to know that, if Sam's hand gets any closer to that pistol on his hip, he's going to be dead on his feet before he even knows what happened."

Dane Olsen leaned in on Longarm. The man had a viciousness that burned in his dark eyes and his breath was fetid and clogged with hatred. "I never liked lawmen," he said. "You bastards wear badges and parade around like you was one of Jesus's gawdamn apostles and you think you can hurt or kill whoever suits you. But you know what? I don't think you're even worth as much as dog shit."

"Dane," Longarm said, fighting to keep his voice calm, "you and your sons are standing right at the edge of hell. Now, you can tell your daughters to get down out of that buggy and come inside or you can do something that will get you buried."

Dane snorted with derision. "Big talk for one man against three."

Longarm threw a glance at Clyde and Jasper. "It's three against three and you have your backs to my deputies, so how do you like those odds?"

The haggard and ugly woman in the buggy jumped up from her seat and swore. "Dane, just simmer down and let's get this done! Ain't no sense in anyone getting shot dead. We'll get the money and leave 'em laughin'."

"You should listen to her," Longarm said to the three Olsen men. "She's making sense. Tell your daughters to get down from the buggy and step into the office. This won't take long and you'll leave town with a sack of cash for your good sense and trouble."

Finally, Dane nodded. "Hilda! Pearl! Get yourselves down here and into the sheriff's office."

Until now, the two young women had been huddled in heavy coats with collars turned up around their faces. Their hair was tucked under slouch hats and heavy coats so that Longarm hadn't been able to see their faces. But now, as they climbed down from the buggy, he could see that they really were identical twins and quite beautiful.

"Step aside and let them pass," Longarm told the Olsen men.

"We're comin' in with 'em," Dane growled.

"No," Longarm shot back. "We need to speak to them in private."

Dane's face clotted with anger and he swore, "By gawd, they're my beauties and I'll be damned if I'm going to let the likes of you or any other man take them inside without me goin', too!"

Longarm knew that he had just a split second to make a decision and that Sam and the other kid were about ready to do something foolish. "All right," he said to Dane. "You can come in with your daughters, but Sam and his brother stay outside. That's the deal you have to take if you want to ever see that two thousand dollars."

Dane trembled with stubbornness and anger. "Deal!" he hissed. "Sam, you and Ollie move over by the buggy near your aunt and stay there until this is done."

"But, Pa," Sam cried, "I . . ."

Dane spun around and backhanded his son hard enough to make him grab a porch post in order not to spill into the mud and snow.

"Gawdamnit, you do as I tell you, boy!"

The first daughter yanked off her hat and stopped between Longarm and her father. She looked up into Longarm's face, deep blue eyes flat and without a trace of humanity. "You're a lucky man today, lawman. You just came close to getting yourself killed."

"Maybe you did, too," Longarm said quietly as his eyes passed to the second daughter. "Go inside and warm up."

"Oh, I'm plenty warm and that money we're a-gettin' is going to go a long ways to keep us all warm for the rest of this winter."

Longarm said nothing as the second daughter stepped up on the porch. She also removed her hat and her eyes lifted upward to meet Longarm's steady gaze. "Who are you?" she asked quietly.

"I'm Deputy Marshal Custis Long."

"Does that mean that you don't work for the sheriff?"

"I work *with* Sheriff Patterson, not *for* him."

"I find that odd."

"You must be Hilda."

"How did you guess?"

"Only two choices and I got lucky," Longarm said, suddenly realizing that he might have said more than was prudent.

"I don't trust you, Marshal Long. And I don't believe a word you say."

"Then why did you come?"

She looked at her father. "Because I do what he tells me to do so I don't get whipped. Does that seem like a pretty good reason?"

"It does," Longarm answered. "Please, let's all go on inside."

"Pa!" Sam shouted. "This don't *feel* right!"

"Shut your yap and watch over your aunt," Dane snapped, pushing inside after his daughters.

Sheriff Patterson was standing behind the door when it swung open and he had a shotgun in his hands. The moment the daughters and their father were in the office he cocked back both the hammers to his scattergun and said, "Just don't do anything stupid. All three of you put your hands over your heads."

Dane went for his gun. Longarm was only a half step behind the man and he clubbed Dane viciously behind his ear, dropping him to the floor, then grabbing his pistol.

Pearl had a stubby two-shot derringer and brought it up in a flash, firing at the sheriff, whose attention had been diverted. The first bullet from Pearl's little pistol exploded in the close confines of the office and Longarm threw himself at the woman as she unleashed her second shot toward the falling sheriff.

Longarm's open palm slapped the side of Pearl's lovely,

hate-twisted face and sent her reeling backward. Hilda jumped between her sister and the gun that had suddenly materialized in Longarm's hand.

"No!" she cried as gunshots erupted out in the street. "Don't kill her!"

Longarm saw Pearl reach into her dress and out came a knife so he knocked it aside and punched the woman right between the eyes, knocking her out cold an instant before her head slammed against the floor. He dropped to Sheriff Patterson's side and saw that the lawman was losing blood fast. Longarm tore off the man's vest and shirt and saw that the wounds were grievous, but likely not fatal.

"I've had some training as a nurse," Hilda said. "We need some bandages to stop the hemorrhaging and we need a doctor!"

"How do I know you're not going to finish what your sister tried to do and try to kill me?"

"I won't," Hilda said, without looking up. "Get me some bandages, damn you!"

Longarm heard a volley of gunshots from outside and he rushed to the front window. Clyde and Jasper were standing over the bodies of Sam and his brother. The aunt had toppled off the buggy and was lying in the snow, blood already staining it bright red.

"Bandages!" Hilda cried. "The sheriff is bleeding to death!"

Longarm saw a dish towel hanging on a rack over near where the sheriff made his coffee. He rushed across the room, grabbed the towel, and tore it into strips. Hilda had already stuck one finger in a bullet hole and now she pushed the dish towel strips hard against the sheriff's wounds.

"Marshal, we need a doctor!"

Longarm grabbed the unconscious Pearl's arm and roughly dragged her into one cell and her father into the other. He slammed both doors shut, found keys, and locked the pair. Then, figuring he had better do as Hilda said, he burst outside into a wild scene of people dashing this way and that.

"I didn't kill the woman," Jasper said, looking a little shaken. "But I pistol-whipped her hard enough to bust her skull. The other ones . . . well, they were going inside and . . ."

"I know," Longarm said hurriedly. "You did fine. Clyde, find a doctor and after you do that find a mortician."

"Did you kill Dane and his girls?" Clyde asked.

"No," Longarm said, "they're locked up, but Sheriff Patterson took two bullets from a derringer and he's losing blood fast. We need that doctor right away."

"I'll find one and bring him back in a hurry."

Clyde took off running as Longarm rushed back into the office, yelling at Jasper to keep the crowd back from the unconscious woman lying sprawled out in the snow and the two young fools who had just been shot dead.

# Chapter 9

"How's he doing?" the old and out-of-breath sawbones asked, tearing open his medical kit and kneeling beside Sheriff Patterson.

Longarm stood looking down at the man and at Hilda, who had managed to stop the bleeding and who now had the sheriff's head cradled in her lap. "Miss Olsen did a fine job of getting the blood to stop flowing."

The doc barely looked at Hilda but gently removed the first bandage and inspected the wound as he turned the unconscious lawman over to better see the damage. "This bullet passed completely through his body and I don't think it hit any vital organs." He then replaced the bandage saying, "Nice job, young lady. Where'd you learn to plug up a hole like that?"

"Long, sad story," Hilda said quietly.

"Let me take a look at this second wound, which struck the sheriff in the shoulder." The doctor again removed a blood-soaked bandage and frowned. He bent and listened to the sound of Patterson's breathing. "Good news! It missed the lung," he said to no one in particular. "Let's roll him this other way so I can determine if the bullet passed through or not. Nice and easy."

Longarm helped to roll Patterson to his other side. The wooden floor was slick with blood. He heard Dane moaning and swearing from his cell but paid the man no mind. Pearl was still knocked out cold and laying facedown in her jail cell.

"Bullet is still in him," the doctor announced. "What caliber weapon fired this shot into Sheriff Patterson?"

"Derringer," Longarm said, noting that the deadly weapon had been kicked under a desk and forgotten. He retrieved the weapon. "A bull-nosed forty-five, Doc."

"Oh yeah, I can't tell you how many of those I've dug out. That caliber does a lot of bodily damage, especially at close range. Who shot him?"

"My sister did," Hilda said unexpectedly. "Pearl shot him with both barrels at almost point-blank range."

"Then I'd say that our sheriff is pretty fortunate not to be dead and your sister is fortunate that she won't be going to trial for murder and then sent to the gallows. Sheriff Patterson has been here a lot of years and he's mighty popular. One of the best men I've ever known."

"They all lied to us."

The doctor glared at Hilda, who said nothing. "Young lady, I heard that you are a nurse."

"I've had some training."

"In surgery?"

"No," Hilda said. "But if you're asking me to help keep this man alive so that my sister doesn't get sentenced to hang . . . then I want to help."

"And you *wouldn't* help if it wasn't for your twin sister?" the doctor asked sharply.

"I didn't say that," Hilda replied. "I said that I haven't had much experience assisting in surgery."

"Well, I need an assistant with a fine touch and I suspect that you can help me once we get the sheriff over to my office just up the street."

Hilda glanced aside at Longarm. "What do you say to that, you gawdamn liar?"

Longarm's cheeks burned. "If you can help the doctor save this man, then that's what you should do."

"I heard you yelling outside and that my kid brothers are dead," Hilda said, eyes filling with tears. "Is Aunt Edna dead? Did your two deputies shoot her as well?"

"No. She was reaching for a shotgun and federal deputy Clyde Peterson knocked her unconscious like I did to your murderous sister."

Hilda looked at her father and sister locked in separate cells. "My father isn't much to brag on but he's always been good and kind to Pearl and me. And I'll tell you this, Marshal, he'll never forget how you deceived us and killed my brothers."

"I don't expect that he will," Longarm agreed. "But I also know that he was in a California prison for trying to hold up a stagecoach and now he's headed for a prison here in Colorado. Your father should be the least of your concerns. Pearl shot a lawman so no matter what else happens, she's going to pay a heavy price."

"So will you and those deputies if my sister or father ever get free."

Longarm looked right into her eyes. "Is that a threat, Hilda?"

"No," she said, "it's a promise."

"Marshal," the doctor said, "we don't have time for this talk. Let's get the sheriff over to my office where I can extract the bullet. If the woman outside lying in the snow needs my attention, she'll have to wait until I'm finished with Sheriff Patterson."

"I expect Aunt Edna might need some stitches in her head," Longarm offered. "She tried to kill my deputies when all the shooting began."

The doctor looked at Hilda. "I've never had to deal with the likes of your family until now, but I've heard that you're *all* thieves and trash."

Hilda's eyes flashed with defiance. "My father and brothers are bent and maybe my sister isn't a saint, but they all work hard and I won't stand you talking that way about them."

Longarm cleared his throat and yelled for Jasper to come in and help him carry the badly wounded sheriff over to the doctor's office because there just wasn't time for angry words. There was a big crowd to disperse, bodies to be transported to the mortician, and things were going to get worse before they got better.

"Hey!" Dane shouted from the jail.

Longarm glanced over to see the man holding his head in his hands, blood seeping through his dirty fingers. "Yeah?"

"I'm going to kill you for what you done to me and my girls."

"You can try if you ever get out of prison," Longarm told the man. "And I expect you heard about Sam and your other son."

Dane's face went white. "What about 'em?"

"They're dead and Edna is hurt. Dane, you should have let your girls come to town and stayed out at the homestead feeding those damned pigs."

"You son of a bitch! I hope that sheriff dies!"

"Let's go," the doctor said.

Hilda hesitated, staring at her father. Longarm's words brought her back. "If the sheriff dies, your sister might hang. Are you going to help the doctor or not?"

In reply, Hilda turned away from the jail cells and marched out the door.

"Let's lift him up easy," the doctor instructed. "He's lost too much blood for us to jostle him and reopen the wounds."

Longarm glanced back at the jail cells, wondering who was going to be able to handle Pearl and her father, given their cunning and open hatred for authority.

# Chapter 10

"Sheriff, how are you feeling this morning?" Longarm asked.

Sheriff Patterson rolled his head weakly back and forth. "I heard what happened. Are the sisters and Dane still locked up in my jail and have my deputies been watching over them?"

"They have," Longarm replied. "But I'm curious . . . why weren't they there yesterday morning when the Olsen family arrived and all the trouble started?"

"One is out sick, another just quit, and the third deputy worked late Sunday night and just didn't get there in time."

"Well," Longarm said, "two are enough to watch over Dane and Pearl for now. The judge will sentence them to prison today and they'll be out of your cell by tomorrow morning. Pearl is meaner than a pit viper and she's threatening all of us."

"She shot me twice at point-blank range, Custis!"

"I know. I was supposed to escort both Pearl and Hilda to California for questioning."

"If the California authorities really need to question Pearl and her sister, they should come to Denver. As for Hilda, I seem to recall that she played a pretty important role in saving my life."

"That's true," Longarm admitted. "She could be pulling the wool over my eyes, but I actually believe that Hilda is far better than the rest of her family."

"So it would seem. After you left here I got to thinking about things and then my wife started crying. Custis, I've decided to retire as of right *now*."

Longarm was quiet for a moment, then said, "That's going to put quite a strain on your deputies."

"I know, but coming this close to death late made me realize that I've pushed my luck to the limit. Like you, I've been in quite a few fights and shoot-outs over the years and damned if I don't think luck often had more to do with it than my skill or brains."

"Are any of those deputies capable of filling your shoes?"

"Deputy Bert Hall has been a lawman for seven or eight years in some tough cow towns and he's hard as nails. Bert doesn't have an easy way about him and he can lose his temper and overreact, but he's got plenty of sand in his craw and he's a dead shot."

"Can Deputy Hall be trusted to do the right thing until Dane and Pearl are sent off to prison?"

"If he stays sober and stays out of the whorehouses, he'll be fine."

"Do you *really* trust the man?" Longarm persisted, not very comfortable with the picture that the sheriff was painting of Deputy Hall. "It isn't going to be easy tonight being around Pearl or Dane and getting them over to the courthouse tomorrow. It's going to take a professional because Pearl and her father are smart and dangerous."

"I can't leave this hospital, but I want you to tell Deputy Hall that I'm giving him the authority to be the sheriff until further notice, and I'll speak to the mayor so he'll be certain to have an immediate raise in pay. Just tell him to be very careful with those two prisoners."

"I sure as hell will."

"Oh," Patterson said, "when you go to see the judge, inform him that Hilda probably saved my life."

"I imagine that they'll still insist that I deliver her to Sacramento for questioning about the murder of Senator Baker."

Patterson stared at him in disbelief. "You'll be expected to take her all the way to California?"

Longarm shrugged. "If that's what my boss and the people in power out in California decide."

"Huh!" Patterson snorted. "That'll be damned interesting. You say you'll be going to Sacramento?"

"Looks like."

"Custis, do you suppose you could check out the prices of houses for me and the missus? Maybe look over a few places and see what you think of Sacramento? I've heard it's beautiful and the climate is sunny the whole year around . . . but it might be too expensive for me and my wife."

"You want me to look at houses so you and your wife can get a better idea if you can afford to live in Sacramento and if it's as nice as you've heard people say?"

"Exactly. I'm worried about those California house prices. We aren't looking to buy anything big or fancy, mind you. We've saved almost a thousand dollars and I'm hoping we can buy something in a clean and respectable neighborhood for that kind of money. My wife says that we'll need three bedrooms and it has to have a nice front porch we can sit and rock on and have lots of trees and a garden."

"Vegetable garden or flower garden?" Longarm deadpanned.

"Both if you can find a place with them."

Longarm laid a hand on Patterson's good shoulder. "If I have the time and I can do it, I will."

"We sure would appreciate that. My missus and I have been talking about going out there to find a house, but it would cost plenty for that extra fact-finding trip. If we could be assured of buying something we liked within our small budget, we'd just pack up and leave as soon as I'm well enough to travel."

"Do you have any kids living here in Denver?"

"Nope. Got a daughter that lives near San Francisco, though. She's mighty anxious for us to move closer. I won't tell her I was shot because she'd just get all worried. But, Custis, it would mean a lot to me and my wife if we could move closer and I think that San Francisco and Sacramento are only a hundred miles or so apart."

"Even less," Longarm told the man.

"Boy, oh boy," Patterson said, clearly excited, "that sure would be nice for us in our retirement."

"If they tell me I must deliver Hilda Olsen to Sacramento, I'll stay an extra day and look at a few houses for you."

"Just . . . just be careful about Hilda," Patterson said quietly. "I know that she saved my life, but maybe she did it hoping to get off the hook and stay out of prison. Maybe . . . maybe she is not as kind as she seems."

"That's a possibility," Longarm admitted.

"And she's beautiful," Patterson continued. "Pretty enough to make a fool out of any man . . . even a lady's man like you."

"Don't underestimate me," Longarm said with a smile. "I've been burned by some beautiful but devious women, and I'm not some lovesick kid who can easily be fooled by a wink and a smile."

"I don't underestimate you about anything," Patterson said quietly. "Believe me, if it wasn't for you I'd be stone-cold dead. I'm alive because of you and that Olsen girl."

Longarm was ready to leave. "I'm going to stop by your jail now and make sure that everything is okay and to tell Deputy Hall that he's now the acting sheriff and he needs to be very careful with his new prisoners."

"He's been pining for my job for a while," Patterson said. "This promotion is really important to him and maybe he will settle into the job and not be quite as rash and cocky."

"Let's just hope that he's able to do what is necessary to get Pearl and her father to the courthouse and then sent off to prison. I think I'll show up in the morning and be part of the escort just to be sure that nothing goes wrong on the way to the courthouse."

"Whatever you think."

"How old is Deputy Hall?"

Patterson considered the question a moment. "I'm not really sure. If I had to guess, I'd say late twenties."

"How did he get to be so good with a gun?"

"I don't know and I don't care as long as he wears a badge," Patterson said. "He's not a killer nor is he trigger-happy, if that is what's concerning you."

"But you said he likes the whorehouses and he is known to have a thirst for liquor?"

"Most young, unmarried men do."

"Yeah," Longarm said, "I suppose you're right."

Patterson winked. "I'll bet *you* have a favorite place when you need to lighten your load."

"No," Longarm said, "I can tell you with all honesty that long ago I made a firm decision never to pay a woman for her favors."

"Well," Patterson said, "you're a big, handsome son of a bitch and I can understand that you wouldn't need to pay for some loving. But Deputy Hall isn't so big or handsome, and I don't make judgments on other single men because I can remember that, when I was young and randy, I had to visit a whorehouse at least once a week or I'd start getting edgy. Of course, what I'm telling you is just between the two of us."

"Of course."

"You know," Patterson said, "Denver is a wonderful place to live and be a lawman. I know that you make more money than I've ever earned, but I also know that you have to do a lot of travel and much of it is dangerous."

"I don't complain."

"Of course not! But listen, Custis, age comes on a law-man quicker than upon most men . . . if they don't get killed on the job or beat up so bad that their brains are scrambled or they're all shot to hell and can't hardly move."

"What are you trying to say?" Longarm asked.

"I'm saying that you ought to think about finding something safer to do . . . and maybe even coming to live in California."

"California!" Longarm barked a laugh. "Now why would I do that?"

"No snow and ice for months on end. No hard winters and you have the Pacific Ocean over there. White, sandy beaches. Beautiful women . . . Oriental, Mexican, and American. I've heard that California is the land of milk and honey and it's where a younger man can make a fortune."

Longarm shook his head. "Seems to me that I recall thousands and thousands of Forty-Niners went to California and almost none of them got anything but grief and regret."

"They were miners! Dreamers! Fools whose heads were filled with visions of striking it rich in the rivers." Patterson's eyes squinted and his voice dropped. "Custis, I'm talking about the opportunities in *agriculture*."

"You mean farming?" Longarm said with obvious distaste. "Pushing a damned plow behind the ass end of a mule or oxen? That sure doesn't sound like much of the good life to me."

Patterson sighed. "I wasn't talking about crop farming. I was thinking about almonds, strawberries, watermelons, and such."

Longarm had endured about as much of this nonsense as he could stand so he patted the former sheriff of Denver on the shoulder and silently headed out the door.

# Chapter 11

"Yeah, sure," Bert Hall said dismissively as Longarm got ready to leave the office, "it's just a woman and an old man so I can handle it tonight."

"I'm sure that you can," Longarm said. "And congratulations on your promotion."

"Way overdue, Marshal," the young sheriff said, kicking his feet up on Patterson's desk. "I should have had this job a year ago. Patterson was a good man in his day, but his day came and went a long time ago."

"I suppose," Longarm said, studying the man from the door. "But there is one thing that a good lawman like Sheriff Patterson had in his favor."

"What's that?"

"He never was arrogant or overconfident."

Bert Hall snuffed with derision. "I know you got a big reputation, Marshal Long, but pretty soon I'm going to have one even bigger. I got a lot of ideas about how to change things in this office."

"I'm sure that you do," Longarm said, trying to conceal his intense dislike for the brash new sheriff. "But you might want to take a little time making those changes."

"And why would that be?"

"People don't like change and I've always thought that the local law here was fair and open."

"Patterson was an old pushover and a pussy," Hall declared, lacing his fingers behind his head and smiling.

Longarm barely controlled his impulse to give the new sheriff a piece of his mind. But instead of getting angry, he gestured toward the two cells. "Looks like your prisoners are done for the night."

"They're asleep. I checked."

"I'll be by about nine thirty in the morning," Longarm said. "That's when the court is ready for the new hearings."

"Don't bother, Marshal. I got it all under control."

Longarm glanced at a clock on the wall. "What time are your deputies showing up tonight to spell you?"

"Hell if I know," Hall said. "I'm fine here just as things are and it seems to me that you're poking your nose in where it isn't needed or wanted. Don't you have anything of your own to do this evening?"

Longarm felt the heat in his face and rather than stride back into the office, jerk Sheriff Bert Hall out of his chair and smugness, he just slammed the door and headed up the street to find a steak and a few glasses of good whiskey.

As soon as he was gone, newly appointed Sheriff Bert Hall got out of his chair and went over to a canvas bag he'd brought in earlier and inside was a bottle of the best whiskey he could buy.

"Celebration time," he said to himself as he turned and

grinned toward the jail cells. "Promotion and celebration time!"

Hall uncorked the bottle and tilted it toward the ceiling. He was a short, but powerful man with a pocked face, and his hair was thin and greasy. Despite his lack of size or looks, he considered himself a rather handsome fellow and now he was *the sheriff*.

"Welcome to your new office, Sheriff Bertrand Douglas Hall!" he said, laughter in his voice. "You finally got what you deserve!"

From the cell, Pearl turned her head toward the scene and said in a bored voice, "You deserve nothing but a bullet in the head, you homely little bastard."

Hall hadn't thought that either of his prisoners was awake, much less that the handsome whore in his cell would actually have the foolish courage to mock him. Taking another pull on the bottle, he sauntered over to stand in front of the cell, smirking and rocking on the balls of his feet. "What did you say, you murdering bitch?"

"Just that you aren't much of a man," Pearl said, standing up and glaring at him.

"You are going to prison for life and if Patterson had died, I'd have loved to have seen your pretty neck get stretched and see those long, white legs of yours dancing in the air. You'd probably have fouled yourself on the gallows, too."

Pearl laughed bitterly. "You really think that you're a hard one, don't you?"

Hall placed his bottle down on a desk and clutched his crotch with both hands. "Long and hard."

"Ha! You're a sawed-off runt and I'll bet your dick isn't two inches long. You probably have to keep jabbing the whores to keep them from falling asleep while you try to get it up."

Hall snorted. "I'm hung like a gawdamn stud horse!"

"Like a mouse!" Pearl chortled. "You got so much, let's see it."

Hall knew that he was being baited, but he also knew that he had more to show than some men so he unbuckled his gun belt, then unbuttoned his pants and dropped them. "See it and weep, bitch."

"First, you had better give me a microscope," she said, squinting and offering a snicker.

Hall took a hold of himself, realizing that he had gotten stiff. He grinned and dropped his drawers to show his stiff manhood. "Like I said, look at it and weep that you never had a taste."

"All right, I was wrong. It's not too bad for a runt like you."

" 'Not too bad'!" Hall looked down at himself and bumped his hips. "It makes women howl."

Pearl smiled. "I could sure use a drink, Sheriff. Going to be my last one for a while."

"Maybe forever," Hall said.

"How about a drink," Pearl said.

"How about you get a drink after you suck my dick?"

Pearl smiled. "Hard dick, hard bargain."

"That's what it is," he said, feeling his heart start to pound and his mouth go dry. "I got the whiskey, you got nothing but prison to look forward to for maybe twenty years."

Pearl sighed. "You're holding all the cards."

"I'm holding something I want you to take into your mouth."

Pearl glanced over at her father, who was snoring on the little bunk.

As if reading her mind, Hall said, "You worried about what your old man might think if he sees you taking me into your mouth? Well, that's a big laugh. You probably did him since you was a little girl of twelve. Right?"

Pearl nodded. "You guessed it, Sheriff."

Hall swallowed hard. "I'm waiting. My offer isn't going to last all night."

"All right. But the drink first, then the other."

"No. You pleasure me first, then the drink. Get down on your knees and put your face tight up against the bars. Do it right now."

Pearl took a deep breath and started to kneel.

"Wait!" Hall choked, voice thick with passion. "Undress first."

"What?"

"Do it!"

"It's my mouth you want so . . ."

"Maybe I want *all* of you," Hall heard himself say in a voice he didn't even recognize.

"I'm going to want more than one drink for what's in your mind," Pearl decided, taking a step back from the bars and folding her arms over her large chest. "Spell it out how this is going to work, Sheriff. Tell me now or you can drink yourself to sleep on the damned floor."

Sheriff Hall's throat was so thick he could hardly speak. He had never been this excited. But the woman was a beauty and she was willing to do whatever he commanded for just a few drinks . . . it was better than his wildest dream.

"Undress. Suck me awhile, then I want you to turn around and put your ass to the bars so I can take you that way."

"No," she said quietly. "You're not long enough and I just won't do it. So go straight to hell."

Suddenly, Sheriff Hall felt he was losing this incredible chance to have something he wanted very badly. "Take your clothes off, Pearl."

"Why?"

Hall's pants were down around his knees. He hopped over to the desk and got the keys to the cell and his gun. He tucked the bottle in his armpit and held up the key. "You do me like I said and I won't blow your brains all over the cell. You can share what's left of the whiskey and I got another bottle."

"You want me bad, don't you?"

"Enough talk! Take everything you're wearing off. Do it right now!"

Pearl stepped back and slowly, tantalizingly let her dress, then one undergarment after the other come down until she stood bare naked before the feverish little lawman.

"Oh my gawd," Hall choked, turning the key in the cell door and taking a long swig of whiskey, then pointing his pistol at the large nipple on her big right tit. "Oh, is this going to be nice! On your knees!"

Pearl slowly lowered herself to her knees. With his pants down he shuffled in closer and closer. He cocked the pistol and placed it at her temple. "Go ahead," he said, jamming his manhood toward her mouth. "You're a whore and you know just what to do."

Pearl took him into her mouth and began what she very well knew how to do. Her mind was racing. Was her father *really* asleep or was he pretending to be just waiting for the chance to get his hands through the bars and around the much smaller man's throat.

And what if Dane was asleep? What could she do now that she had this one chance? The barrel of his gun was poking her hard over the ear and his manhood was pushing deep into her throat.

"Don't hurry it," he said in a husky voice. "Do it slow. Lick it awhile!"

Pearl heard him cock the hammer of his gun back and press it even tighter against her head. She moaned as if she was enjoying having his stinky dick in her mouth and tried not to gag.

"That's right. That's right!"

Pearl could feel his legs and hips began to tremble and she knew that he was going to come in her mouth soon . . . very soon. And if he did that . . . once he did that she was finished. He'd have been satisfied and back out of the jail and never even giving her a drink.

It is now or never, she thought.

She heard a scrape or rustle in the next cell and looked past the sheriff's thrusting hips to see her father wildly motioning for her to back the little bastard up into his reach.

"Oh," Pearl moaned, shoving her face hard into his crotch so hard he had to take a big step back. "Oh gawd!"

"Don't stop!" he said as he groaned, "don't . . ."

Whatever his next words were, they died as a pair of powerful hands shot through the bars and gripped Sheriff Hall's throat, instantly crushing the windpipe. Hall's head snapped back in the grasp of Dane's powerful fingers and was slammed over and over against the bars until the skull was a wet mass of blood, hair, and bone.

Pearl jumped up and spit in the little man's face. She drove her knee into his crotch again and again while her father had the lawman pinned to the bars. Then, picking up the pistol that had slipped from Sheriff Hall's fingers, she took aim and shot his manhood off.

"Let's go!" Dane said. "Get those keys."

Pearl Olsen spat again on the corpse at her feet and wiped her mouth with the back of her arm. She staggered out of the cell but not before picking up the fallen whiskey bottle before it could drain out. She drank long and hard and then she grabbed her clothes and started dressing.

"Unlock this gawdamn cell!" Dane shouted in anger. "You're a whore! You can get dressed later!"

"The little bastard was almost right, Pa."

"What the hell do you mean!"

"He said you had probably been screwing me since I was twelve . . . but you started when I was just ten. Never touched your sainted Hilda, though. Why were you raping me and not her?"

"Gawdamnit, there's no time for this shit! Unlock my cell!"

"So," Pearl said, "you won't tell me why I was your little whore and Hilda became your little saint!"

"Pearl, you bitch, I . . ."

Pearl didn't hear the rest of whatever he was going to say because she shot him right through the eye and watched his head jerk backward and then his body crash to the cell floor.

"Payback at last," she said with a big smile.

Out in the office she found that other bottle of whiskey—it really had been of the highest quality—and then she took a few guns and a fine Winchester rifle. She filled the now-empty canvas bag with the bottle, her new weapons, and plenty of ammunition.

Just as she was about ready to slip out of the office and disappear into the night, she had a thought and returned to the cell where the sheriff now lay in a pool of blood around his crotch.

"Got some money for me?" she asked, frisking the body and knowing that her dead father didn't have a cent to his name.

Hall had ten dollars and change. Not much, but more than she'd sometimes demanded and received for doing what she'd done to him.

"A whore deserves to be paid," she said, wondering what would be said when they found their new sheriff stone-cold dead with his pants down around his knees and his dick shot off. And what they'd say when they saw Dane still locked in the next cell, shot in the eye.

Pearl took another swig of whiskey, planted the cork, and slipped away in the night. If she could have, she'd have found and killed the big United States marshal this very night but that would be pushing her luck. She was pretty sure that Sheriff Patterson was still in a hospital and for a few moments considered trying to track the man down and cutting him open for the lying he'd done to get most of her family killed.

"The big federal marshal was the one that came up with this lie," she said to herself. "He's the one I want and from what I've heard, he's going to be taking Hilda to Sacramento. I can get even with him there or on the way. I can think it out and do it right and slow."

Pearl slipped out into the night, thinking that justice was coming to those that deserved it for what had been done to the Olsen family and it would start by eliminating of United States Marshal Custis Long. She knew hard men from here to Sacramento who would help her eliminate Marshal Custis Long . . . and if her sister didn't help and display her family loyalty, then maybe Saint Hilda would also have to die.

# Chapter 12

The next morning after a leisurely breakfast at his favorite café Longarm headed for the sheriff's office, and when he was yet a block away he saw a big crowd gathered out in front.

"Damn," he swore, "I knew something bad was going to happen last night because of that stupid, arrogant sheriff!"

Longarm broke into a run, being especially careful to avoid the icy patches where a man could take a hard spill. When he arrived at the office he shoved his way through the crowd. The office was packed with men; some were in the jail cell and others were crowded around the desks and everyone was gawking and talking excitedly at once.

Longarm drew his gun and fired it into the plastered ceiling, killing the talk.

"Everyone other than who needs to be here get out!"

The crowd turned on him. A self-important Denver business man snapped, "You're a *federal* officer so what gives you the authority to tell anyone what to do?"

Longarm didn't bother to answer but instead roughly shoved the man toward the door. "Get out!"

There was a good deal of grumbling and swearing, but Longarm was so forceful with the crowd that they finally pushed outside to join the other spectators.

"I'm Deputy Rollins," one of the men said, stepping forward and swallowing nervously. Rollins still had peach fuzz on his cheeks and looked badly shaken. "I worked for Sheriff Patterson and I'm the one that came in first and saw what happened in here last night."

"Is that a fact," Longarm replied, grabbing the young man by the sleeve and dragging him aside. "What the hell happened here last night?"

"The back of Sheriff Hall's head got smashed to jelly and from the way his neck is looking, it's plain that he was strangled."

Longarm swore under his breath. "And the next thing you're going to tell me is that Pearl Olsen and her father got away?"

"Pearl did, but Dane Olsen was shot dead."

"By the sheriff before he died?"

"I have no idea. But both men are dead and the woman is gone."

Longarm would examine Hall and Olsen in a few minutes, but right now he needed to think about what he'd just heard. How could the two men have died while the woman escaped?

"I can't figure it out at all," Rollins said, sounding almost panicked. "It makes no sense."

"There's got to be a reasonable explanation," Longarm told the young lawman. "Pearl looks strong, but she couldn't have strangled Hall without the help of her father. The sheriff was short, but solidly built so that means that Dane somehow got to the sheriff *through the bars*. When you arrived, was Dane's cell locked or unlocked?"

"Locked, but the cell where we were holding the Olsen woman was unlocked and I found the ring of keys on the floor about where we're standing. Marshal, it was a terrible sight. When I saw those bodies, I almost soiled my pants."

"Just calm down, Deputy. I need to examine those bodies before they're removed by the undertaker. Is that him in there draping both bodies with sheets?"

"Yes, sir. But before you go have a closer look, there's something I really think you ought to know."

"What's that?"

Rollins cleared his throat. "When I arrived, the front door to the office was closed but not locked from the inside. I didn't think too much about that although Sheriff Patterson had been a real stickler for keeping the door locked if a prisoner was jailed overnight."

"That just makes sense," Longarm replied, "but I'm not sure what it has to do with anything, given that Sheriff Patterson has retired. What . . ."

"Please, let me finish," Rollins insisted. "When I stepped inside, I saw Bert lying in a pool of blood."

"Of course you did," Longarm said, growing impatient, "you said his skull was caved in from behind."

"But what I need to tell you," Rollins insisted, looking off with embarrassment, "is that Bert's pants were down around his ankles and his . . . his cock was shot off."

Longarm leaned in closer, not sure if he'd heard the deputy correctly. "What!"

"I'm telling you what I saw and what you're going to see if you pull his pants down the way they were when I found Bert dead on the cell's floor."

"So you pulled Sheriff Hall's pants up?"

"Yep. And I buttoned them and fixed his belt."

"Why?"

The deputy's hand passed nervously across his face and he seemed to have trouble answering the question. Finally, he blurted, "I just . . . well, I just didn't think it was right that everyone would be looking at what had been his manhood before it was shot off. Bert Hall was a hard man but *no man* deserves to have people gawking at something that horrible."

"I see. You thought he deserved better."

"I did," Rollins admitted. "Was I wrong?"

"No," Longarm told the earnest young deputy, "you did the right thing. I would have discovered what had been done to him anyway, but there is no point in everyone seeing something that bloody and awful."

Rollins expelled a sigh of relief. "Marshal, do you think that Pearl could have . . . well, done something that horrible to the sheriff?"

"Yes," Longarm answered. "But maybe even more important is that I'm beginning to think that your newly appointed sheriff did something very foolish and dangerous last night that cost him his life."

The deputy looked totally confused. "So you're telling me that Pearl shot off Bert's . . . well, you know . . . but she *didn't* strangle him or bash his head in."

"No, Dane Olsen did that."

"Then who shot Dane Olsen?"

"I'm not sure yet. As he was being strangled, Sheriff Hall might have managed to throw his gun up over his head or twist around just enough to shoot Dane who had a stranglehold on him from behind."

"Marshal, Bert was shot dead-center through his right eye."

Longarm considered this small but important bit of information. "Deputy, turn around so that your back is to me."

"What?"

"You heard me, turn around."

When the deputy hard did as ordered, Longarm stepped in close. "As I recall, Sheriff Hall was right-handed."

"Yes, he was."

"Just pretend *you* are being strangled and you have your gun in your right hand. How would you use it to stop me from strangling you from behind?"

Rollins lifted his thumb and extended his finger to imitate a pistol. "Well," he said choosing his words carefully, "the only way I could have turned my barrel on you close behind me is to have raised my gun over my left shoulder and . . ."

"And you would almost certainly have shot me in the *left* eye," Longarm said, finishing the deputy's thought.

He released his hand from Rollins' throat. "So if Dane Olsen was strangling the sheriff from behind and through the bars, we have to conclude that it would have been almost impossible for him to shoot Dane through his right eye."

"I understand."

"So Pearl shot her own father," Longarm concluded, "and then she shot Sheriff Hall's manhood off before she left the office. Are any rifles missing from the rack or any other weapons or ammunition?"

"I didn't think to look."

"Then you should do that right now while I'm examining both bodies."

"Yes, sir."

The deputy shook his head. "What kind of woman would

do something like that to a man who had already had his neck snapped and the back of his head bashed into jelly?"

"A woman who absolutely hates men," Longarm answered. "Hates them so much that she even killed her own father. Once in a great while in my work I've met women like Pearl, and they're so filled with hatred that it doesn't matter who the man is . . . he deserves to die."

Deputy Rollins considered this a moment then asked, "Do you think that Pearl killed her father because she was beaten and raped as a girl?"

"There is every possibility that is exactly what happened."

"What about her sister, Hilda?"

Longarm saw that the mortician had placed both dead men on stretchers and was instructing helpers how to lift and remove the bodies. "Deputy, we can talk later. Right now I need look at those bodies."

"Yes, sir."

Longarm's inspection was quick but necessary. He examined Sheriff Hall first, not bothering to pull down the man's pants because they were soaked with blood. Clearly, Hall had died of strangulation followed by a broken neck and extensive head injury.

The mortician said, "Marshal, there's blood, hair, and bone on the bars between the cells."

Longarm glanced up and nodded. "I need to take a quick look at Dane's body before you cart him off to the mortuary."

"Take all the time you need; these two won't mind and neither will I. I'm just glad that Sheriff Hall was able to put a bullet through that bastard's eye before his neck was snapped."

Longarm didn't bother to tell the mortician that Pearl

had been the shooter. A few minutes later, he was staring at what had once been Dane's eyeball but was now just an eye socket pooled with black and caked blood.

"I've seen enough."

"I should think so. Glad these two won't have an open casket funeral although I make more money that way."

"I understand that Sheriff Hall had no wife or children . . . no family of any kind."

"That's right," the mortician said, "and if I may be blunt and honest, he didn't have any friends, either."

"Take them away and bury them fast," Longarm told the man in the black suit.

"My name is Waldo Utley and you, Marshal Long, have provided me with a good deal of bodies and business in the last two days so I thank you."

"You're welcome."

"And, if I may say so, I hope that I retire or die of old age before it is *your* turn to show up in my funeral parlor."

"Amen, Mr. Utley. Amen." Longarm turned to the few remaining people in the office and said, "I want everyone out of here except Deputy Rollins."

A fat, disheveled man appeared in the door, clearly out of breath. "I'm Deputy Nolan! What's going on here!"

Longarm studied the deputy who was in his forties. "Glad you could finally show up on the job, Nolan."

"I've been feverish," the man said, coughing to emphasize his point. "But I'm here now and . . . oh my gawd!" He stared at the corpses. "What happened!"

"Where is your badge, Nolan?"

"Right here," the deputy said, pulling his badge out.

Longarm took it from his hand and said, "You no longer work here. Go back to wherever you came from."

Nolan's jaw dropped and he looked wildly around the office for help before he blurted, "You can't fire me, you're a federal marshal!"

Longarm grabbed ex-deputy Nolan by the seat of his pants and propelled him out the doorway, slamming it in his wake.

"Marshal," Rollins said, "if he isn't going to work here, who's going to help me out until a new sheriff is hired?"

"For the time being, I will."

"What should I do now?"

"Get a bucket of hot, soapy water and a mop, Rollins. Clean up the cells and the bars because I'm going to find Pearl and bring her back to this jail. And this time," Longarm added, "she'll go before a judge and be sentenced to hang for murder."

"Yes, sir! But . . . but what happened to the other sister?"

Longarm waved his hand dismissively. No point in going into any long explanation about how he'd allowed Hilda to sleep in his bed last night while he slept on his couch. And today, Hilda was being watched over by his landlady, on the strict promise that she would not try to run away or do anything rash or stupid.

"Sheriff Rollins," Longarm said, "we'll talk at greater length later. Right now, I need to visit the judge and afterward see if I can find out what happened to Pearl Olsen."

"Can I let anyone in here before you get back?"

"After you clean up the cells, I don't see why not if they have a purpose. But no morbid gawkers. And I'd also advise you to keep your mouth shut about what happened and what we talked about. There's going to be an investigation and you might have to take an oath as a witness. So just keep things to yourself."

"Thank you for telling me that. I'll stay quiet."

"Good. I'll be back later . . . hopefully, with Pearl in handcuffs."

Longarm headed for the courthouse. He knew Judge Ely very well and was sure that the man had already heard about the jail cell murders that had taken place the previous night. Judge Ely would want some answers and explanations, and Longarm would provide them in his usual concise manner. But after that, he would be on a womanhunt.

A few minutes later, Judge Ely and Longarm were alone in the judge's quarters. "So," Ely said, "that's the long and the short of it?"

"Yes, sir."

"What about the sister? Do you think she might have played some role in the murder of Hall and her own father?"

"Impossible."

"And why is that?"

"Because," Longarm said. "She wasn't in jail last night."

"Oh," the judge said, raising his bushy eyebrows. "And where was she?"

Longarm cleared his throat. "She had saved Sheriff Patterson's life with her nursing skills and so I let her stay at my apartment under my watch last night."

"All night? Alone with you?"

Longarm shifted uncomfortably. "Listen, I know it sounds wrong, but . . ."

"It was wrong," the judge said. "Marshal, you can't keep that woman in your apartment."

"She wasn't under arrest," Longarm countered. "And I'm pretty sure that I'm going to be ordered to deliver her to Sacramento so that she can go before an investigating committee regarding the murder of Senator Taft Baker."

The judge, a distinguished-looking man in his late sixties, shook his head and paced back and forth in his small study for a few moments before he stopped and stared at Longarm. "If you are not very, very careful, you could get yourself involved in something that could ruin your reputation and career."

"I understand."

"Do you? Do you really?"

"Yes, Judge, I do."

"All right then, just go out and find this Pearl Olsen if she is still in Denver. But I'd strongly advise you not to give your full trust to Hilda Olsen until you are absolutely sure of her motives and intentions. She might be even more evil and cunning than any of the rest of that viperous clan."

"I'll keep a close eye on her."

"And by the way, I understand that there was an older woman that was pistol-whipped."

"Yes, that would be Pearl's Aunt Edna and she along with the wagon disappeared during all the commotion and confusion."

"She recovered and drove away?"

"I don't know what happened, but she's gone."

"That will bear some looking into."

"Yes," Longarm agreed, "it will. If I don't find Pearl in Denver, I'll ride back out to the Olsen homestead and see if either Edna or Pearl is there."

"Be careful."

"Always. Don't worry, Judge. I'll keep my guard up."

The judge almost smiled. "I understand that those sisters are quite beautiful. That being the case and knowing you, Custis, I'm afraid that you're going to keep more than your guard up around Pearl Olsen."

Longarm pretended to be shocked moments before he left the judge's chambers and stepped outside the courthouse. The sky was dark and he figured it was going to storm and drop fresh snow.

But what really mattered right now was finding Pearl Olsen because he had a feeling down deep in the marrow of his bones that she was not through killing and that he might be her next target.

# Chapter 13

Pearl Olsen poked her head around the corner of a building and saw Longarm emerge from the courthouse. She had a rifle and guns, yet something told her that even if she was able to shoot and kill the federal marshal, she would soon be run down and caught.

"I'd never make it out of this town alive," she said to herself. "And besides, there is Hilda."

Pearl eased back from the corner and shivered in the snow that had packed between the buildings. What she really needed was to pick the time and the place to kill Marshal Long . . . a time and a place where she was certain she could do it and survive.

She was cold and poorly dressed for this freezing weather and she knew that her long blonde hair and voluptuous figure were going to be impossible to disguise. The entire city was abuzz with the rash of killings that had taken place in the last two days, and Pearl was pretty sure there might even be a bounty on her head.

So what to do?

There was only one thing to do and that was to leave Denver and make her way westward to Sacramento. That, she was quite sure was where she would find the marshal and most likely her sainted sister. In Sacramento she had many friends that would help her . . . if she paid them their pound of flesh.

But how to get out of this town! That was the difficult part and if she didn't come up with a plan very soon, she would be forced to either rob someone or put herself in great danger.

So Pearl stood shivering in the dim corridor between two cold, brick buildings, trying to think of some way to escape and then to have the time to plot her revenge. She decided that she had no choice but to wait until darkness and then to find a home and kill its occupants. Denver had its wealthier sections and maybe she could find a mansion with some old, rich people who rarely went out in this bad weather. She could kill them, hide in their home for a few days . . . maybe even a week, then take whatever money and jewelry she could find and pay someone well to help her get away.

But could she physically endure waiting until darkness? She felt so cold that her teeth were rattling and her thin cotton dress and worn shoes offered nothing in protection against the icy grip that was slowly squeezing the life out of her. Why hadn't she taken a few minutes before she fled the sheriff's office to grab a heavy coat and a hat? She had never been so miserable and the idea of hiding out in this foul weather seemed out of the question. By evening, she would be so numb that she would not be able to move and she might even have frozen to death.

Pearl was afraid, really afraid that she might die before

she could find a mansion and seek its warmth. She was not only freezing, but she was feeling weak from hunger.

*My gawd,* she thought, gripping her rifle and starting to take aim on the marshal, *I'd rather die of a bullet than slowly freeze to death.*

And then she saw someone who might just be her ticket out of town. It was a middle-aged snake oil peddler and he was hitching up his colorfully painted medicine wagon to two skinny horses and preparing to leave.

Pearl's eyes narrowed as she watched the peddler. She had seen his kind many times before. They were charlatans, hawking their medicines and spewing their lies that only the most desperate or gullible swallowed. Her father had once nearly killed one of them when the man had come to their homestead promising a cure for Aunt Edna's many illnesses. Dane had beaten the peddler almost unconscious, then taken his bottles of "the cure" and drank them declaring that the medicine was pure corn liquor with maybe some turpentine or horse liniment to give it a look and medicinal scent.

Dane and her brothers had gotten very drunk that night and the peddler had barely been able to climb into his wagon and leave.

Why not? Pearl decided. *I can hide in his medicine wagon and no one would ever think to look inside. Maybe there are scissors inside and I can cut my long hair, and there are bottles of dark elixirs that will dye what hair I keep so that I would never be recognized, even by Hilda.*

Pearl managed a thin, bloodless smile. Here was her answer! This peddler was her deliverance. She would wait until the man was on his wagon seat and then she would come out of hiding and ask him for a ride out of town. And given that she was wearing such a thin dress, he would see the curves of her body and there was no doubt that he would invite her to join him in exchange for sexual favors.

Pearl almost laughed out loud. A medicine man was always traveling from town to town and she would make sure that his path led toward California. And if this peddler had other ideas, then she would kill him and become a *medicine woman*.

*By gawd, I will sell fools medicine by day and my body by night and I will be a wealthy woman by the time I reach Sacramento!*

# Chapter 14

Longarm escorted Miss Hilda Olsen into the Federal Building and then up the stairs to Billy Vail's private office.

Billy came to his feet, his expression grim. "I heard about
the jailbreak and killings that took place last night, but no
details."

"Sheriff Hall is dead as is Hilda's father."

Billy studied Hilda. "I'm sorry about the death of your
father."

"So am I," she said, looking pale. "But even though he was
my father, I know that he was not a good man, nor is my twin
sister. What I would like is for Pearl to be found and arrested.
It's my hope that she will not be shot down but will instead
serve time in prison and someday be redeemed."

"Of course," Billy said. "This must be very hard on you."

"I've seen it coming for years," Hilda said in a small
voice. "And I had no love for my stepbrothers. They were
deadly young men and I knew that one day they would either
be shot or hanged. I am concerned about my aunt Edna, and

I understand that one of the deputies in this office knocked her out cold and that she fell from our wagon into the snow."

"Yes," Billy said, tapping some papers on his desk. "I have it all down here in a written report. During the excitement, the woman recovered and slipped away. Do you think that she returned to your father's homestead?"

"I don't know," Hilda replied. "But it is likely. She had no other place to go."

"Then maybe that is where your sister is to be found."

Hilda shrugged. "Possibly, but Pearl has other choices."

"Mind expanding on that?" Longarm asked.

"Pearl is very smart and resourceful. She won't be easy to capture and she might decide she would rather die in a gunfight than be sentenced to prison for many years or even hanged."

Billy nodded. "We don't know if she committed a murder in that jail . . . but we suspect that she might have. Any thoughts on that, Miss Olsen?"

"None that I care to share with you," Hilda said quietly.

"Custis," Billy said, "everyone in the office wants to know what happened in the sheriff's office. Do you mind addressing them?"

"No," Longarm answered, "I don't. Will you assign men to help find and arrest Pearl?"

"I will," Billy promised.

Longarm took Hilda's arm and led her out of the office. Every deputy and clerk in the big office was standing in anxious anticipation of hearing what he had to tell them.

"Fellow deputies," Longarm began, eyes covering the room, "this is Miss Hilda Olsen and I'm sure that all of you have heard what happened at the sheriff's office. Deputies Jasper White and Clyde Peterson along with myself were able to apprehend Dane Olsen and Pearl Olsen. Two Olsen men died in a shootout just outside in the street and Sheriff Patterson was wounded severely."

Longarm continued, "Miss Hilda Olsen was responsible for saving Sheriff Patterson's life and was therefore not jailed along with her father and sister. What you may *not know* is that sometime last night, the interim sheriff, a man named Bert Hall, was shot to death along with Dane Olsen."

There was a quick murmur of surprise. Longarm waited a moment then said, "We know with certainty that Pearl Olsen had some role in the deaths of one, possibly both men and I have asked Marshal Vail to put every available deputy in this office on the hunt for Pearl Olsen. One of the sheriff's deputies, a young man named Rollins, has been asked to fill in until a permanent sheriff is hired and he has told me that a Winchester rifle and several pistols along with boxes of ammunition are missing. Therefore, we should consider Pearl to be armed and extremely dangerous."

A deputy asked, "What about the old lady that disappeared?"

"Her name is Edna Olsen and she probably found a way back to the Olsen homestead," Longarm replied. "This woman pulled a shotgun and was going to open fire on Deputies White and Peterson so she should also be considered to be very dangerous."

"When and where do we start the hunt?" a deputy asked.

Billy Vail stepped forward. "Finding and capturing Pearl Olsen is our highest priority, and I want men to check the train depot and every stage line in town. Pearl Olsen is desperate and smart. She might be trying to hitch a ride with a wagon freighter and she might also try and steal a horse and some supplies in order to get as far from Denver as quickly as possible. So check all the liveries and stables. Ask on the streets if anyone has had their horse stolen in the last few hours."

"There are thousands of horses in Denver," one of the deputies said pointedly. "And at least a dozen liveries and that many freight and stagecoach lines."

"I know," Billy answered. "That's why I'm going to spend the next hour with you men to make sure that every possible means of escape is covered. Custis, I'd like you to jail Miss Olsen and ride out with me out to the Olsen homestead along with Deputy White."

"Hilda isn't going to try and escape," Longarm said. "She doesn't need to be put behind bars."

"I'm sure that's true, but I can't take any chances. When you return, you can remove her from jail confinement if you can promise me that she will not disappear like her sister."

"I'm not going to try and run away," Hilda said, looking upset. "How in the world could I do that with all of your deputies looking for my twin sister? If I ran, I'd probably be shot by mistake."

"Good point," Billy conceded. He turned back to Longarm. "Where can she stay until this hunt is over?"

"My landlady will watch over her and I promised the woman that she would be compensated for her time and trouble. Ten dollars would be fair."

"All right," Billy said, reaching for his wallet, then peeling off some bills and handing them to Longarm. "It'll be quicker and easier if I just pay that out of my own pocket."

Longarm took the money. "Can Hilda stay put in your office while we make the assignments?"

"Fine idea," Billy said.

Longarm took Hilda back into Billy's office. "There's hot coffee over there on the table. This won't take long."

"Then what?"

"Then you have to promise me that you will stay with my landlady until I return from your homestead."

"I'll do that if you promise me you won't shoot Aunt Edna down on sight."

"I'll make that promise, but if she opens fire on us, I can't promise anything."

"I understand."

Longarm left the woman in the private office and went out to join Billy and his fellow deputies. Every deputy knew Denver like the back of their hands and a list was quickly drawn up of stagecoach line offices and liveries, then equally divided. Billy ended up by saying, "Deputy Peterson, you're in charge of the train depot. That would be the easiest and most likely avenue of escape, but for those very reasons I don't expect that Pearl will attempt to board the train."

"All right," Deputy Peterson said, looking a little disappointed. "How long do I have to camp out at the depot?"

"Until we've caught or killed Pearl."

"Understood."

When the office had emptied of deputies, Billy led Longarm over to a corner of the room and in a low voice said, "I'm concerned about Hilda not being who we think she is."

"You mean our helper and willing witness."

"Yes," Billy said. "I just don't know how she can stand by while her sister is being hunted as a possible murderess."

"Maybe it's like she says, she just wants Pearl to be arrested and sent to prison so she has some chance of being redeemed."

"Maybe," Billy said. "Let's hope so. But be very careful."

"How soon are we leaving for the Olsen homestead?"

"Within the hour. Oh, one other thing I have to tell you."

"I'm listening."

Billy frowned. "I received not one but *two* telegrams today. One was from Sacramento and the other from my boss in Washington, DC, and they both told me that they wanted Pearl and Hilda Olsen in Sacramento as soon as possible."

"Can't that at least wait until we capture Pearl?"

"No," Billy said, "I'm afraid not. And to be honest, I'm not confident we'll be able to capture her alive . . . if at all. So what I'm telling you is that you have to get Hilda on the train bound for California tomorrow morning no matter what happens regarding her sister or Aunt Edna. Understood?"

"Yeah," Longarm said, not at all pleased. "But—"

"It's out of my hands," Billy interrupted. "And maybe we'll get lucky and capture Pearl before the day is over."

"Maybe," Longarm said, not really believing it.

# Chapter 15

When the snake oil peddler put the whip to his team of horses and drove up the street, Pearl knew she couldn't wait a moment longer. If the man was wary or if he'd heard about Pearl being an escapee and possibly a murderess, then she would have to try and kill him then shove his body down where it couldn't be seen and drive out of Denver with her hat pulled down low. But if he hadn't heard of her escape, then it would make things much easier.

Pearl left her hiding place and watched the medicine wagon move up the street, and then she walked swiftly, trying not to think about how her feet were frozen and her hands shaking badly. When she saw the medicine wagon round a corner, she cut through an alley and ran through the snow, stumbling and falling twice but managing to arrive in front of the wagon. She stepped out into the side street in front of the wagon and threw up one hand while the other gripped the Winchester.

"Help!" she croaked, voice cracked from the cold. "I need help!"

The snake oil peddler hauled on his reins and his wagon ground to a stop in the mud and the icy slush. "Are you a woman?" he asked, squinting hard at her.

"Yes, and my husband is trying to kill me!"

The peddler's eyes widened. "Well, how the hell come?"

"He . . . he says that I'm a wanton woman and no damn good." Pearl began to sob.

"Ma'am, I don't think I can help you out."

"But you must!" Pearl cried. "Just give me a lift out of town so that I can get away from him or he'll murder me for certain!"

"I'm heading south," the man said, "down to Pueblo."

"I have friends in Pueblo! They'll take me in and . . . and I'd be so grateful. Please, kind sir, show me just a little charity!"

"I'm not an especially charitable man," the peddler admitted. "You got any money?"

"No, but my friends in Pueblo will gladly pay you for this small service. If you are already going that way, this will cost you nothing."

"Well . . . well, all right," the man said after long deliberation. "But are you really as wanton as your husband says?"

"Even *more* than he says." Pearl removed her wide-brimmed hat to show her long blond hair. She stuck out her chest to let him know that, under the heavy coat, there were two lush breasts.

The snake oil peddler gulped, then licked his lips. "You must be freezin' to death, ma'am. Come on up here and we'll get you warmed up. I got some medicine that we can both share in this cold. We'll be feelin' better in no time at all!"

Pearl clapped her hands together and allowed him to climb down from the wagon and help her up to the seat, aware that he kept his hand on her bottom longer than necessary. When he joined her, she leaned in close and said, "You've saved me."

"Not yet I haven't," the peddler said, looking around nervously. "Any chance that your husband is waiting with a gun just up the road?"

"None at all. He's dead drunk right now. And I have his rifle."

"Nice rifle," the peddler said, glancing at the stolen weapon. "Know how to use it?"

"No, do you?"

The peddler nodded and said with pride, "I shoot rabbits for supper when I can. Shoot coyotes, too, and skin 'em for money. I'm a good damn shot."

"My husband can't shoot anything," Pearl admitted. "He's the worst shot in the world."

The peddler's shoulders sagged with relief. He slapped the lines down hard on the backs of his two horses. "Get along, girls!" he shouted. "We can make it twenty miles before sundown."

Pearl beamed at him and he said, "Reach behind you through that little wooden door and grab one of my medicine bottles and then pop the cork. We're going to enjoy ourselves in this bitter cold and there is nothing more in the world that I like than my own medicine and a young, *wanton* woman."

Pearl laughed merrily and reached for a bottle.

# Chapter 16

Longarm, Billy Vail, and young Deputy White rode though heavy and wet flakes of falling snow, hats pulled down over their faces. Their horses plodded along through the slush, and the sun was just barely a faint light in the western sky.

"There is no doubt that Edna drove the wagon back here," Longarm said as they followed the rutted wheel tracks clearly still visible in the snow. "I guess the question is . . . did Pearl somehow manage to get a ride back out to the homestead with her?"

"If she did," Billy said, tugging the woolen collar of his coat up closer to his face, "then we might be facing two ambushers."

"We can get close, thanks to the poor visibility," Longarm told his boss. "But we'd better spread out and flank the cabin. I'll get off this horse and be ready if they bust out on the porch and open fire."

"I hope it doesn't come to that," Billy said, face tight with worry. "Shooting women isn't something I even want to consider."

"Just remember that Pearl probably shot off Sheriff Hall's manhood and then put a slug through her own father's eye. And I'll just bet you that old Aunt Edna is every bit as ready to kill all three of us."

"I know that," Billy conceded. "Jasper, peel off to the left and have your rifle ready to fire."

"Yes, sir."

"I'll take the center position," Billy said.

"No, you won't," Longarm countered. "You're too wide a target."

"Are you implying that I'm *fat*?"

Longarm managed a frozen grin. "Billy, let's just say that I'm a little quicker and younger and I should take the middle. Also, I don't have a wife to worry about."

Billy reluctantly nodded. "I hope we can do this without any more bloodshed."

"Don't count on it," Longarm said as Billy reined his horse off to the right.

Longarm drew his saddle carbine from its boot and levered in a shell. He removed his gloves, shoved them deep in his coat pockets, and pulled his hat down tight. Right now, he was thinking that warm, sunny California sounded just about like heaven.

At thirty yards he hauled in his horse, dismounted on stiff legs, and dropped his reins. His rented gelding stood still, forelegs planted wide in the snow, head down and blowing little puffs of steam from its nostrils. Even with a snowfall, the Olsen homestead smelled of hog shit and decay. The only sound was that of the hogs snorting in their big shed and pen. There was no dog to sound the alarm and the cabin's windows were shuttered. Longarm saw that the team of horses that had pulled the wagon after the Denver shoot-out now stood with their heads low, still hitched.

"Edna Olsen!" he yelled, his voice brittle with cold. "It's Marshal Custis Long! You need to step out on the porch with your hands in the air."

Silence.

"Pearl, if you're in there with her, you'd better just surrender and face a judge because we're not going to leave without either of you."

After several anxious moments, the door opened a crack and through it poked the twin barrels of a shotgun. Longarm threw himself forward into the snow and the shotgun's double blast passed just over his head but struck his horse, which bolted in pain and began plunging through the snow back toward its Denver livery stable.

Longarm stayed buried in snow as Billy and Jasper opened fire at the doorway. When they had unleashed at least ten shots each, Longarm threw up his hand and shouted, "Hold your fire!"

He could see the shotgun's barrel was laying on the door-step, and just as he was about to climb out of the snow, he saw the door swing open and there was Edna, spread-eagled on the porch emptying her pistol. Longarm threw himself headfirst into the snow a second time and more rifle fire erupted on either side of him.

The top of Edna's head was suddenly no longer gray but a mass of dark blood, and the woman wasn't moving. "Stop!" Longarm shouted.

Almost immediately, the penned hogs caught the scent of fresh blood and began squealing with excitement and hunger. Longarm pushed to his knees then to his feet, rifle aimed at the cabin just in case Pearl was waiting for a close-up kill. But nothing moved up ahead, and finally Longarm mounted the porch and grabbed the barrel of the shotgun and tossed the weapon into the snow.

He leaned his Winchester against a porch post and drew his pistol. Longarm crouched low and stepped inside gun moving back and forth, but he knew at once that Pearl wasn't inside.

"Come on in!" he shouted back to Billy and Jasper and stepping around Edna's body.

Once inside the cabin, Longarm found a lamp and lit it. The place was littered with dirty clothing and empty tin cans and extremely filthy. It stunk so bad that Longarm took only a few minutes to check the bedrooms and after finding nothing of interest, went back outside where the air, while cold, was at least clean.

"She's of no help to us now," Jasper said, staring at the dead woman in the doorway. "I wonder whose bullet took off the top of her skull."

"Mine," Billy answered, seeing the revulsion on his young deputy's face. "There's no doubt that I'm the one who killed her, is there, Custis?"

"No doubt at all."

Jasper looked very relieved. "Well, I would have shot her if you hadn't first," he said quietly. "Now what do we do?"

Longarm considered the question. "We feed the hogs, burn this place to the ground, and take the old woman's body back to Denver for burial." He looked closely at Billy. "That sound about right to you?"

Billy was staring down at the body. "It does," he said at last. "And we ought to turn the hogs loose or they'll just starve to death or start fighting and eating each other."

"Do you really think they'd do that to each other?" Jasper asked.

"Yeah," Billy said. "My father raised hogs and they're smart, but they're meat eaters and they won't all just curl up together and starve to death. The strong will eat the weak and then the last of them will fight to the death."

"Billy," Longarm said a few minutes later when they were alone, "I thought you told me that your father was a book-keeper and you grew up in a city . . . not a hog farm."

"That's true," Billy said, "but I did know a man who raised hogs and he told me a story about a pen of them that ate each other after the farmer killed his wife and then shot himself. Besides, I think that it was Jasper's bullet that took off the old woman's head, and if I'm going to tell him one lie, I don't suppose a second one much matters."

"Oh," Longarm said, not understanding the logic and not interested in trying to figure it out. "Well, let's get this over with and get back to town. This storm might get worse and we don't want to be out on the road after darkness."

"Good thinking. You set the cabin on fire. Jasper and I will haul Edna over to the wagon. At least we won't have to hitch it up and you won't have to walk back to Denver."

"That's right," Longarm said, "I'd momentarily forgotten that my horse was shot and ran off. I hope he wasn't hurt too bad."

"Me, too," Billy said, "because if it dies or has to be put down, then the liveryman will have every right to expect that the federal government pay him for a replacement and, frankly, my budget is slim right now."

Longarm took a deep breath and plunged back into the cabin. He grabbed up the lamp and moved from room to room, setting things on fire and making sure that there was nothing inside that should be saved.

There wasn't, and by the time he was finished and flames were licking at the falling snow, Billy and Jasper had Edna in the back of the wagon covered up with horse blankets.

"The hogs," Longarm said, tromping over to the pen and the little shed.

At the sight of him approaching, the hogs went wild. The bigger hogs were snorting up a storm, the smaller ones squealing as if their throats were being slit. Longarm ducked into the shed, found nothing to feed them, and unlatched the gate. The hogs stood still for several minutes and then they rushed outside, snorting and chuffing, smelling fresh blood but eyeing the rising inferno.

"Let's get out of here," Longarm said, jumping up into the Olsen wagon and slapping the lines on the backs of the team. "Yah! Yah!"

The horses jolted ahead and Longarm drove them out of the yard toward Denver. The snowfall had intensified and the wind picked up. Longarm slapped the lines down on the horses but he knew they were too weak and underfed to move faster. Billly and Jasper rode up beside him and Billy shouted, "We've got company behind us!"

Longarm twisted around and saw every last pig on the place following them. Well, he thought wryly, if this isn't going to be the sorriest spectacle that ever drove up the streets of Denver . . . a dead old woman and a herd of starving hogs tracking old Edna Olsen's blood trail.

# Chapter 17

Longarm was so cold by the time that they arrived back in Denver that he tumbled off the wagon into the snow. The Olsen hogs had found some garbage at the edge of town and were gone, probably looking for even more. Longarm stood and waved Billy Vail on, yelling, "I'll take care of Edna's body! You and Deputy White head on home."

Neither man objected. Longarm dragged the half-frozen corpse out of the wagon and, trying to keep from falling, slipped and slid his way up to the funeral parlor. Aunt Edna couldn't have weighed more than eighty pounds, but with the footing so treacherous, it was a job to get her to the front door and then drop her on the porch.

He hammered on the door a few times, discovered that it was unlocked, and let himself inside. The snow was blowing so hard that he grabbed Edna and slid her right through the doorway and into the parlor.

Mortician Waldo Utley burst into the nicely furnished

front parlor with its wine-colored carpeting and polished maple furniture. "Good gawd, you killed the old woman!"

"We had no choice. The old gal opened up on us with a double-barreled shotgun."

"Did you get hit?"

"No, but my rent horse did and he ran away. I expect he's probably back at his livery, if he didn't bleed to death."

Utley looked at the body and the snow melting on his rug and then he pulled back the cover and stared at the body. "My gawd! The top of her head is missing."

"There was no time to do anything but open fire on her before she killed one of us," Longarm explained. "At least the blood has coagulated in the cold and isn't running all over your floor."

"Help me get her into a tub," Utley said. "I can't take the chance of her messing up my fine carpeting. That looks especially gruesome and that's saying something for a man in my profession."

When they had the body in a tin tub, Utley swung a curtain closed and went back out into the parlor. "It must have been awful riding out there and then having to shoot the old lady."

"It was," Longarm admitted. "We decided to burn the Olsen cabin to the ground and we set loose their hogs that followed us all the way back to Denver, then scattered into the alleys searching for food."

"Why did you burn the Olsen house down?" Waldo Utley asked.

Longarm shrugged. "I don't know. But the place just reeked of evil things and evil people. I guess Billy and I felt equally as strong about wanting it gone forever."

"Well," the mortician said, "I can understand that and

I've gone into homes for bodies and had the same, dark, menacing feeling of evil. What about Pearl Olsen?"

"No sign of her at the homestead. I think she's managed to find a way out of Denver, but I haven't had time to check with the others."

"And Hilda?"

"I'll be escorting her to California very soon. Maybe even tomorrow."

Utley managed a smile. "A thousand miles or more in a nice, warm railroad coach with a beautiful woman and then you get to visit a place where the sun is shining and there isn't any snow or ice. Not a bad reward for what you've just gone through."

"I hadn't looked at it like that, but I suppose there is some truth in what you're saying."

The mortician walked to the front of his parlor and stared out at the driving snow. "Did you know that Sheriff Patterson and his wife are my good friends?"

"No."

"Well, they are. My wife also likes his wife very much. Mitch Patterson is trying to talk me into moving to Sacramento and he told me that he'd asked you to look at some real estate for him."

"That's right," Longarm said. "If I have the time."

"Well," Utley replied, "I'd like to have you look for a home for Gertrude and myself as well."

Longarm was wet and shivering and in no mood for this conversation. "I'm not a damned real estate broker, Mr. Utley!"

"Of course you aren't, Marshal. But as long as you are sort of checking things out in California, please keep me and Gertrude in mind. We'd prefer something a little nicer than the sheriff and his wife can afford. Three bedrooms at least and . . ."

Longarm threw up his hand. "Mr. Utley, I've had a really bad day and I'm frozen to the marrow of my bones. I'll look around in Sacramento if I can, but right now I just need to go back to my apartment, change out of my frozen clothes, have a big glass of whiskey, and maybe draw a tub of hot water."

"Of course! Of course! How unkind of me to bother you with a request at a time like this. Forgive me and I sincerely want to thank you for all the business you've brought me in the last few days."

"You are welcome," Longarm said, turning for the door.

"I won't be able to bury any of them until the ground unfreezes," Utley said almost as an afterthought. "And I've already been told that they are to go into the pauper's area of the cemetery and that no one will pay for marble headstones."

Longarm turned at the door. "Nobody liked them or cares how they are buried."

"True enough. However, I feel it is my professional obligation to at least put their dates of death and estimate the year of their births."

Longarm heaved a deep sigh. "Mr. Utley, you do what you think is best. I really don't care. Right now I'm going to take the Olsen team of horses to a livery and unhitch them and feed them because those two poor, starving beasts are standing at death's door. And I'm going to see if the horse I rented has returned and if he is going to recover. And after all that, I'm going home to take that bath."

"You should rest a day before you board the train to California with Miss Hilda Olsen," the mortician suggested.

"You should have a good day of rest with her and enjoy her company."

"I'll give that idea careful consideration, Mr. Utley, and when I return I hope I can provide you and the sheriff with a little real estate information concerning homes in Sacramento."

"We would all be *most* grateful! The sheriff and I are . . . well, we are a little concerned that with that beautiful woman and the warm, sunny weather you might *never* return to Denver."

"Is that a fact?"

"Marshal, let's be frank, the temptations you are going to face in the weeks to come are enough to change the life of any man, so what I'm suggesting is not really so unlikely, is it?" the mortician asked, raising his bushy eyebrows and offering a sly wink.

Longarm didn't dare smile because he figured his frozen lips would crack, but he had to admit that the mortician had a valid point.

While driving the wagon back to Denver he had developed a good deal of sympathy for the two skinny Olsen horses. The outlines of their ribs and knobby backbones were plain to see and they were unshod and shaggy beasts. So after he exited the funeral parlor he took care to lead the team and wagon down the empty street through the heavy snow to the livery where he did business.

"Jeff! Open up!" he yelled into the storm.

But Jeff was either out to eat or fast asleep so Longarm unhitched the two horses and led them into the barn where he dried and rubbed them down with empty grain sacks. He found two clean stalls and fed them grain and hay. When that was done, he checked the other stalls and was greatly relieved to see his saddle horse had returned, been doctored, and was standing dry and steady, munching hay.

"Sorry about the shotgun pellets," he said.

Back outside he bowed his head to the blowing snow and made his way through nearly empty streets until he reached his apartment building. Barging inside, he knocked on his landlady's door.

"My gawd!" the old woman who owned the building said. "You look as white as a ghost!"

"Have you ever seen one before?"

"A ghost?"

"Yeah."

"I see the ghost of my dear, departed Egbert every night," she told him a little defensively. "And if you laugh at that I'll get a frying pan and bend it over your frozen skull!"

"Easy, Penelope," he said, looking past her to see Hilda sitting on a horsehide couch. "You know I just like to tease you."

"You don't look to be in condition to tease anyone," the landlady said, eyeing him from head to toe. "Can I make you some hot coffee or tea?"

"No, thank you." Longarm gestured to Hilda. "Let's go."

Penelope said, "I believe you promised me ten dollars, although I have to admit that I've really enjoyed Hilda's company. She's had an amazing and difficult life, that one. And so lovely!"

"Look," Longarm said, "just add the ten dollars to my rent next month. Right now I need to get some dry clothes on and get some whiskey into my belly."

"Tea or coffee would serve you far better, Custis."

"I know, but I'm weak. Let's go, Hilda."

"You be nice to that girl," the landlady warned. "Remember to be a gentleman."

"I will," Longarm said over his shoulder as he stomped up the stairs to his upper-floor apartment with Hilda close behind.

"The key is hidden under the mat at our feet. I'm so frozen I'm not sure that I can even bend over for it. Will you?"

"Of course."

Hilda got the door opened. "You need to get out of that coat and those frozen stiff pants," she said. "Where is the whiskey and glasses?"

"Over there above the stove." Longarm peeled off his heavy coat, then his gun belt. His fingers were numb and bloodless. He fumbled with his buttons, and Hilda, seeing his difficulty, came over to help. Let me do this."

Longarm was only too glad to let her help. Soon, he was undressed and shivering even harder as he threw down a few swallows of good whiskey.

"I hope you don't catch pneumonia and die," Hilda said, looking worried. "What happened out at the homestead?"

"Your aunt Edna opened fire on us with a double-barreled shotgun. She hit my horse and we had to kill her. Afterward, we searched the house but there was no sign of Pearl."

"I knew she wouldn't be stupid enough to go back there."

"Well, she sure won't now because we burned the place to the ground."

"Why!"

"It was a bad place, Hilda. It just was . . . bad."

Hilda poured herself a drink and watched Longarm try to find some dry clothes. "You should go to bed and cover yourself up with blankets."

"I'd get warm faster if you undressed and got into bed with me," he offered.

Hilda studied his drawn, haggard face for a moment, then tossed her own whiskey down and began to undress.

"You're really going to do it?"

"You are very, very cold," Hilda said. "And you're right, I can help you warm up much faster with the heat of my body."

Longarm risked cracking his lips with a smile. "You've got a big heart." A moment later when she was undressed, he added, "And some very big and lovely breasts."

"Get into bed and be still and quiet."

Longarm climbed into bed and she slid in beside him. He heard her gasp when he pressed his stone-cold body up tight against hers but after stiffening for a moment, she pulled his face up against her neck and draped one of her long, shapely legs over his body, cradling him.

"I've died and gone to heaven," he whispered into her hair. "Can we just stay like this forever?"

"Don't be silly," she said softly. "We have to go to California tomorrow."

"Tomorrow is a long time from right now." Longarm could feel his manhood sprouting like a weed in a garden, big and fast. "I . . . I don't know if I can do this for very long," he confessed.

"I know what you want."

"And?"

"You can have me after we warm up and have another drink."

"I don't need another drink."

"I do." She climbed out of his arms and poured herself a generous glass of whiskey. "Want more?"

"I sure do."

Hilda poured a second glass and sat down on the bed beside Longarm. "I'm not going to try and tell you I'm a virgin . . . because I haven't been since I was fifteen."

"Your father?"

"No, one of the stepbrothers . . . then both. They overpowered me and had their way with me many times over the years."

"Did you tell Dane?"

"No."

"Why not?"

"Because I knew that he would kill them and then maybe he'd kill me. I was his perfect little princess and saw what he was doing to Pearl and didn't want that to happen to me if he felt I had fallen from his imaginary pedestal."

"So you just let your brothers . . ."

*"Stepbrothers,"* she corrected. "And yes, I had no choice. My father would have made all of us pay in ways that I won't even try to describe to you."

"I'm sorry," Longarm said.

"Me, too." She took a long pull of whiskey and when she looked at Longarm, there were tears in her eyes. "I'm telling you this so that you understand why and how I can forgive Pearl for being who she is. She never had a chance and I think if she had not been there I would have turned out exactly like her."

"I'm not convinced of that."

Hilda sniffled. "You don't know anything about me or Pearl. But I've told you now that I'm anything but pure so that you don't have any guilt."

"Not sure I would have even if you hadn't told me about the stepbrothers," Longarm admitted.

Hilda let him empty his glass and then she emptied her own. She slipped back into bed and this time she pulled him on top of her and then into her. Longarm lost himself in her heat and soon, he felt like a strong man again as he took her gently and then passionately. When it was over, he rolled off and lay staring at his ceiling.

"This is amazing, Hilda."

"What is amazing?"

Longarm swallowed and took a moment to form his thoughts into words. "This has been an awful day from start to finish and now, with you, it's turned out to be a great day."

"That's true," she said, kissing his cheek. "And isn't it more important not only for a day but for our lives that they end well?"

"It is." He looked closely at the woman. "What do you think will happen with Pearl?"

"I don't know. We look exactly alike but we think very differently."

"I sure hope so."

"We do, I promise."

"Will she try to find and kill me for what I did to your family?"

"It's very possible."

Longarm had to ask one more question. "She wouldn't hold it against you as well, would she?"

"I don't know," Hilda confessed. "But she might."

"I'll protect you," Longarm vowed. "I will protect you with my life."

Hilda kissed his face. "You are a good man and I know you are very, very capable, but you aren't cunning like my twin sister. Neither am I. If she puts her mind to it, there is very little that will save us from her vengeance."

Longarm didn't believe that, but looking into Hilda's shimmering blue eyes, he could tell that she believed it and that was almost scary.

# Chapter 18

Two miserable days later when they neared the town of Monument, Colorado, some fifty rutted and frozen miles south of Denver, Pearl decided that she'd had enough of the snake oil peddler, Vernon Teague. The night before in shabby little hostelry where Vernon had gotten uproariously drunk with some of his customers, he'd come to bed reeking of his medicine and tried to rape her. She had managed to grab a bottle and bash him in the head, knocking him unconscious.

The next day, hungover and not remembering anything, Vernon had complained about how he must have hit his head on the bedpost.

"That's right," Pearl said, "you fell hard and were passed out cold."

"My head sure does hurt," he complained. "And I've got a splitting headache."

"It's called a hangover," Pearl told him. "It always happens when you get sloppy drunk."

"I don't need you telling me how much to drink."

"No," Pearl said, hiding a smile, "you sure don't."

Since escaping Denver in the medicine wagon, Pearl had been sizing up the situation and had come to the conclusion that she couldn't afford to spend another night with Vernon. And besides, if she had to listen to another bad joke or boasting of Vernon's seduction of some poor, sick woman on his long selling route, she knew that she would go crazy or put a knife in his neck.

"Another hour," Vernon said, trying to make his horse pull a little faster, "and we'll be in town. I know a place there where we can stay cheap. The husband is away working for the railroad a lot and Mildred and I have had some good times in her feather bed. Gonna be a little awkward showing up with you, but maybe we could make it a threesome."

Pearl blinked in surprise and disbelief. "Are you serious?"

"Sure!" Vernon said, uncorking a bottle and upending it. "I think Mildred would enjoy it and I know I would. How about it if she agrees?"

In reply, Pearl tore the bottle out of his hand and drank.

"Aw," Vernon said, sensing her disgust, "Mildred is a little old but she's a frisky thing between the sheets and she really goes wild when she gets a bottle of my medicine in her . . . wild as a skinny little weasel."

"She sounds like a woman that needs a new husband."

"Well," Vernon said, "as a matter of fact, she has said she'd like to divorce her husband and go traveling with me. But I think Mildred would get on my nerves pretty quick and I don't believe she could take the pounding of these bad roads in daytime and me pounding my meat into her at night. Know what I mean?"

Vernon tried to reach under Pearl's coat and cup her breast, but she slapped his hand away. "Pay attention to your driving."

"Aw, come on," he wheedled, "you owe me for giving you a ride out of Denver and tonight I mean to collect my first installment, if you get my drift."

"I get your drift and you're right, I *do* owe you, Vernon."

"Glad you realize that," he said, clueless as to her true and deadly meaning.

Pearl drank some more medicine, her mood as dark as the sky. She decided that she would have to get rid of Vernon before they reached Monument and that meant it had to be very soon. "Vernon, how much money do we have with us?"

"What the hell is this 'we' business?"

"I meant do you have enough money to get us a good, clean room in a hotel when we reach Monument? I saw you hiding it in that old mail sack."

He gave her a suspicious look. "You don't miss much, do you?"

"No," Pearl admitted, "I don't."

"Well, I got me eighty-nine dollars and change in that pouch but I'm not going to spend it foolishly on a hotel room when we can stay with Mildred for free."

When Pearl said nothing, Vernon continued, "Damnit, woman, why should we spend good money when Mildred is willing to take us in for the night and even let us eat at her table!"

"What if her husband is at home this time?"

"Hmmm," Vernon Teague mused, "as a matter of fact, he has been there a time or two. But we can find that out and if he's there, we can stay in a spare bedroom."

"I don't want to stay there," Pearl said. "I want a good hotel and a good meal and warm, clean sheets."

"Damnit," Vernon whined, "only two days and already you're making demands on me!"

"Well," Pearl said, "here's another. I have to take a shit and I'm not going to do it right here on the road so pull over into those trees."

Vernon leaned out of his medicine wagon and craned his head backward. "Nobody in sight. Just hop down and shit. No need to drive through the snow into those trees."

"Do it, gawdamnit!"

The sharpness of Pearl's voice widened the peddler's eyes with surprise. "Hellfire, woman! You sure got a burr up your pretty ass today. I'm the one that's got a knot on my head and a hangover, not you."

Pearl just glared until he swung his wagon and the single big, gray horse off the road and through the snow toward the distant copse of trees while he grumbled, "Sure is wasted time and effort steering through this snow just for you to take a shit."

Pearl didn't say a word but sat on the seat beside the man until they were in the trees. She jumped down and marched around the wagon. She'd placed her rifle and guns in the back and she was going to get them right now.

"Hey," he called, cackling with his sick humor, "I've got to piss and I'd like to see you shit! How about I join you?"

The man was demented! Pearl unlatched the rear door to the medicine wagon, hauled out her Winchester and levered a bullet. She didn't care if Vernon had just heard the sound or not.

"Sure!" Pearl called. "Come along and watch me if it makes you randy!"

"By gawd it will!"

Vernon set the brake, jumped down, and started to

unbutton his trousers. He was fumbling with the buttons when she stepped out from behind the wagon and shot him twice at close range. The first bullet knocked him up against the wagon wheel and his mouth flew open in a silent scream. The second slug hit him a little higher, right about where his sick, shriveled little heart must have been. Vernon did scream just before that second shot and it sounded like a terrified rabbit caught in the jaws of a coyote just before it died.

"Well, Vernon," she said, placing the Winchester up on the driver's seat and then dragging his body a way off from the wagon into the trees, "I guess we won't do the old threesome tonight after all with the little weasel woman."

Pearl found a little shovel that Vernon kept in the medicine wagon. She used it to pitch a mound of snow over the dead man and then she climbed up into the wagon, released the brake, and drove the wagon back onto the road.

Someone was bound to ask her in Monument and later in Pueblo why she was driving the wagon and where was Vernon Teague? Pearl thought hard about her response to that expected question.

"I will just tell them that Vernon died after drinking whiskey instead of his medicine," she said aloud. "I'll say that he died and was buried in Denver, all nice and proper and he willed his wagon and the secret to his medicine to me, his loving sister."

Pearl laughed into the cold late afternoon air and reached around to get a fresh bottle of the stuff. She would get a room tonight and every night to come because she could sell snake oil and fake medicine as well as Vernon and the fool had even told her of the exact ingredients.

"Waaaa-hoo!" she called, a long cloud of steam pouring

through her nostrils. "I got me some money, a new profession, and a horse and wagon. I'm going to Sacramento and I'm going to have some fun on the way! Waaa-hoo!"

And then she remembered Custis Long and how he and his deputies had killed her brothers. Most likely, he'd even killed Aunt Edna by now. Suddenly, the delight she'd felt a few moments earlier about killing Vernon and taking over his money and possessions vanished to be replaced by a cold, murderous desire for revenge.

# Chapter 19

"Can we just say that we're man and wife so that people on the train won't keep staring and having dirty thoughts?" Hilda asked as they stood in the depot getting ready to board the 106-mile run up to Cheyenne.

"If you'd feel more comfortable with that, it's fine with me. I'd have thought that by now you'd be used to people staring at you," Longarm said. "You're really quite a looker . . . but then you must know that."

"I've never liked attracting attention. Pearl does, but not me."

Longarm heard the train's whistle blasting to announce immediate departure. He picked up two valises and led the way to the boarding platform. Because he traveled so often on the Denver Pacific Railroad he knew almost all of the people who worked the cars and coaches.

"Good morning, Marshal," the attendant said as he took Longarm's ticket and punched it then tried to hide his surprise when Longarm gave him a second ticket for Hilda's fare. "My, my, what a *lovely* lady."

"Thank you," Hilda said. "We got married."

Longarm had forgotten the attendant's name but he wouldn't soon forget the look of surprise on his face. "Well, isn't that just fine!" the man said, grinning from ear to ear. "Congratulations! Going on a honeymoon?"

"That's right," Hilda said, beaming like a new bride. "We're going all the way to Sacramento."

"Well, I do declare. I will make sure that you and the marshal get extra special attention on this short run up to Cheyenne. I sure will."

"Thank you."

Longarm let the attendant help Hilda up into the train and heard the man whisper to him, "Nice, Marshal, *really* nice."

"Thanks."

Since the run was short they didn't have a sleeping compartment, but the attendant made sure they were taken to the first-class coach. "You two lovebirds just enjoy the scenery."

"We'll do that," Longarm said, feeling guilty for the betrayal. When he returned alone from California, he'd have to confess to this man and probably many others that it had all been a lie of convenience.

The ride up to Cheyenne was quiet and uneventful. Longarm saw that the snow had drifted higher than fences in some places, blown by a nearly constant and freezing wind. In Cheyenne, they made a quick change and were soon on their way west, heading over the Laramie Mountains toward Rock Springs, Elko, and then Reno and finally Sacramento.

"Did you ride the train to Sacramento when you were with Pearl?" Longarm asked as their train struggled up the mountains.

"Yes."

"Why did you go to California and how did you meet and go to work for Senator Taft Baker?"

"Long, complicated story," Hilda said. "And not one that I care to talk about right now."

"This is going to be a long trip so maybe you can talk about it later."

She patted his thigh. "I don't think you should count on me telling you what happened to the senator while we were working as his house staff and personal attendants. Mostly, it was a boring job."

"I would find it a fascinating story."

Hilda shook her head. "Let's just . . . just enjoy the trip and let the cards fall where they may when we reach Sacramento."

"Fine, but I have to ask you something. Do you expect to be arrested for the senator's murder?"

Hilda stared out at the pines draped with snow and the bleak, pewter-colored sky. "I have no earthly idea," she finally managed to say. "None at all."

Longarm studied her profile and thought about what she'd said and not said. He knew that he was starting to get very attached to Hilda and understood that this was not good or healthy. If she and Pearl had murdered the senator, then Hilda would either go to prison for many years . . . or possibly even be sentenced to the gallows because of the prominence of the victim.

*Better to just keep an emotional distance on this trip,* he decided, *if I possibly can.*

* * *

When they finally left Reno and began to climb up the eastern slope of the snow covered Sierras, Longarm took a little more interest in the surroundings. He had often traveled as far as Reno and he was very familiar with the Comstock Lode, but rarely had he been sent all the way to California.

"I understand that laying this track over the Sierras was mostly accomplished by the Chinese."

"The transcontinental railroad involved one hell of a race," Longarm said, as the train crept across a trestle and then through a snow shed. The drop-off was impressive and far below was the Truckee River, rimmed with ice. "The Union Pacific used mostly Irish labor to fight its way across the Great Plains . . . a lot of former Civil War veterans. They were tough men and they faced the elements and the Indians as well as prairie fires. But laying track between Sacramento and Reno was an even greater challenge. Most engineers after the Civil War who looked at the grades and elevations didn't even think it could be done."

"How come they brought in Chinese?"

Longarm stared down at the river far below. "Well, this fella named Charles Crocker was one of what was dubbed "The Big Four" and I don't remember the names of the other three. All of them were rich and when they couldn't get sober, reliable workers to start up the western slope out of Sacramento, they hit upon the idea of hiring Chinese who were not especially big or strong men, but they didn't drink and they worked well together without always getting drunk and fighting."

"I understand that caused a lot of resentment."

"It did, but the Chinese didn't care and neither did Crocker."

"Did many Chinese die?"

"I'm sure that they did. In accidents and some froze to death in the winter up near Donner Pass. They were buried without markers."

"How sad."

"Yes," Longarm said, "but I'm sure that their fellow Chinese honored and remembered them all."

Hilda stared out the window. I can't believe that they could lay track up this high and on such narrow roadbed."

"Well, they sure did, and I understand that the western slope was so steep that they had to blast ledges in the sides of cliffs with Chinamen hanging in baskets setting the fuses. They did it with dynamite and later with nitroglycerine. It took them months so they hopscotched off the summit and worked on this side of the Sierras so they wouldn't be slowed by the Donner Summit Tunnel."

"What a story," Hilda said. "This is a beautiful but kind of frightening ride over these snowy mountains. "

"I know what you're feeling," Longarm admitted. "It is a bit unnerving to look straight down into these deep gorges. But I'll tell you one thing, when the tracks met at Promontory Point in Utah, it linked the east to the west and suddenly, people could come and visit this country without the hardship of doing it by horse, steamship around Cape Horn, or by wagon."

"Who do you think won the race?"

Longarm thought that an interesting question. "I'm not sure if either the Central Pacific coming out of Sacramento with Charles Crocker in charge of the Chinese or the Union Pacific with its Irish and veteran army of workers won. Both railroads were given enormous sums of money and land as incentives and all the major owners probably got even richer than they had been before. But the transcontinental railroad was an epic and unifying force for the entire nation. I'm just glad that I didn't have to swing those hammers or lug those millions of railroad ties."

"That does sound like backbreaking work. Did the Chinese all go back to China after the railroads met?"

"Most did and what they took back probably made them rich or at least important people in their Chinese towns and cities. But a lot of them stayed, primarily in San Francisco's huge Chinatown."

"What are you going to do when we get to Sacramento?"

"I have to turn you over to the authorities," Longarm confessed. "And then I'm going to look at some homes for sale in behalf of some people in Denver."

"They want to move to Sacramento?"

"They sure do," Longarm answered. "Sheriff Patterson and his wife sound like they are ready for some nicer weather and so is the undertaker, Mr. Utley."

"The one that is putting most of my family in the ground," Hilda said quietly.

"I'm afraid so."

"I always knew that it would come to something like this. Pearl and I used to talk about how we were cursed from birth."

"I doubt that to be true."

"Oh, it *was* true! But that's in the past now. Let the dead rest in peace and speak no more of their sins and sorrows."

Longarm glanced sideways at Hilda, struck by those thoughts. He saw that her expression was sad and he wondered if her sorrows were only beginning after the Sacramento authorities took her into custody.

# Chapter 20

"Marshal," the burly Sacramento sheriff said, "we appreciate you bringing Hilda Olsen back all the way from Denver. We're just disappointed that you couldn't bring her sister along as well."

"No more than I am," Longarm told the man. "Pearl Olsen is a killer for sure."

"So is Hilda," the thirty-something sheriff snapped. "I hope you weren't fooled by her beauty and innocent looks."

"I wasn't," Longarm told the lawman as they stood outside the jail. "But . . ."

The sheriff cupped his crotch in one hand and barked an obscene laugh. "I can see that she got to you a bit on the trip out from Colorado! Not surprising. Did you get to screw her a few times?"

Longarm's jaw clenched and he held his silence.

"Oh, come on, Marshal Long! You must have jumped her bones at least every hundred miles between here and

Denver in a sleeping car. I'll screw her if I get half the chance before she swings at the end of a noose."

"And what," Longarm asked, his voice low and brittle, "is *that* supposed to mean?"

An elderly and well-dressed couple passed and the sheriff tipped his hat to them and said, "Nice day, Mr. Raney. Good to see you both out and enjoying a little sunshine and exercise."

"It's always a nice day in California," the dignified-looking gentleman replied, giving Longarm the once-over. "I understand that one of the Olsen murderers has finally been returned to us."

"That's right!" The sheriff grinned. "This is United States Marshal Custis Long from Denver. He brought Hilda Olsen in today on the train."

"What happened to the other one?" Raney angrily demanded. "This town wants to see a *double* hanging. None of us will be satisfied with anything less than both those bloody bitches dancing at the end of a hangman's rope."

Longarm was taken aback by this callus remark. "Sir, Miss Hilda Olsen hasn't even been charged with the senator's murder, much less been tried."

"Humph!" Mrs. Raney snorted. "Trying either one of them is a waste of our hard-earned taxpayer money. Those heartless whores seduced and then murdered a fine senator and a good friend of ours. Why, Senator Baker might have one day been the president of the United States!"

Longarm took a deep breath. Telling this couple that he didn't appreciate Hilda being called a "heartless whore" wasn't going to change anything and would just result in angry words.

"But we have a problem," the man said. "Judge Gratton's

mother took ill down in San Diego and he left on the packet last night."

Sheriff Felton scowled. "Well, how long will the judge be in San Diego?"

"Could be a month or two!"

"Damn!" Felton swore. "That means that I'll have to keep the prisoner fed for a hell of a lot longer than expected and it will sure eat a hole in my office budget."

"Maybe they can find a replacement," the woman said. "This is a very big and important trial. People will come from all around given how much Senator Baker was loved."

"That's right," her husband said. "Maybe we'll get a replacement for Judge Gratton, but we won't find that out for at least a couple of weeks. And as for your jail budget, I'm sure those of us on the city council will give you some extra money for your prisoner if you run short."

"I'll feed her light," Felton said. "Bread and water. She's got enough meat on her bones to do fine until we get a judge and she goes to trial."

"Trial won't take long," the woman said. "Everyone knows that those two sisters killed the senator for his money. They're as evil as Satan and that's a fact!"

"You're right about that, Mrs. Raney. Right as rain."

Longarm had been listening to all of this and now he was ready to leave. If the trial didn't start for weeks or even months because of Judge Gratton's problems, that just gave him a little more time to try to find Pearl, who was probably the sole killer.

"Sheriff," Longarm said while tipping his hat to the vindictive old woman, "I'll be taking a meal."

"Try the Red Bird Café just up the street," the man advised. "Good food and reasonable prices."

"Thanks."

As Longarm walked away, he heard Mrs. Raney say to the sheriff, "Every day that Hilda Olsen lives is a travesty and an affront to God the Almighty who is going to smile when Hilda Olsen is sent to burn forever in hell."

"Amen to that," the sheriff said in hearty agreement.

Longarm spent the next two days looking at neighborhoods and asking about prices and housing availability. From what he could see, Sacramento homes were a little more expensive than they were in Denver. He quickly learned which were the safest and most desirable parts of town. Longarm knew that the newly retired sheriff and his friend the undertaker wanted to buy something modest but appealing.

"Marshal, send your Denver friends my way," a smallish man who specialized in home sales told Longarm. "I'll find them what they're looking for at prices they can well afford. I know Sacramento like the back of my hand and I'll treat them honestly and courteously."

The real estate man gave Longarm his business card and added, "After looking at our beautiful city whose climate is almost unsurpassed have you thought about relocating to Sacramento?"

"No," Longarm told him. "But I could imagine myself living here when I get old."

"Our time passes all too quickly, Marshal. Don't wait to enjoy our paradise until you have one foot in the grave."

"Wouldn't dream of it," Longarm replied.

After leaving the real estate man, Longarm wandered down to the docks along the Sacramento River, watching big paddlewheel steamers plow their way up and down the big river. This was quite a fine town, he decided, while wondering if a trial date for Hilda had been set by the court and jurors were being selected. Hilda would, of course, be appointed a public defender and Longarm hoped that whoever that was had some competence and experience.

By the third day in Sacramento, Longarm was bored at looking at real estate and the bustling river-port town. Sacramento was beautiful and it seemed prosperous although all of the easy-to-get gold had long since been extracted from the nearby foothills and neighboring streams. He knew it was time to buy a return ticket and get back to Denver, but he just wasn't quite ready to do that and he understood the reason why . . . Hilda Olsen. Sure, she was probably as guilty as anything and deserved a quick trial and a noose or at least a long prison sentence for murder . . . *but what if she was innocent*? What if Pearl, who had not hesitated for even an instant in killing Sheriff Bert Hall and even her own father, had been the sole killer of Senator Baker?

Longarm decided that he needed to make sure that Hilda at least got a fair trial before he headed for home. And he wanted to know that Hilda was being treated properly or if the sheriff here was abusing her. Longarm had finally remembered the man's name . . . Sheriff Dub Felton.

So fifteen minutes later, Longarm stepped back into Sheriff Felton's office and saw the man sitting at his desk reading a newspaper. From the look on Felton's face when he saw Longarm, it was clear that the unexpected visit was not welcomed.

"Well, well," Felton said, lowering his newspaper. "I would have thought you would be in Denver by now."

"I've been sightseeing and scouting out some real estate for friends that want to move out here," Longarm explained, his eyes moving past Felton to the cell where Hilda lay on a bunk with her face turned away as if she were asleep.

"Given the shitty winters you Colorado people endure, I can't imagine why anyone stays back there," Felton said, eyes tracking back to his newspaper. "Any *other* particular reason you haven't gotten back to Denver and your work?"

"No, not really," Longarm said, forcing a smile and moving in the direction of the cell. "Just enjoying the California sights and weather."

"Well," Felton growled. "I think you should get back to work and try to find Pearl Olsen instead of wasting time in Sacramento."

"She's being hunted by a lot of lawmen," Longarm explained, sidling up to the cell and throwing a glance at Hilda, who had turned to looked at him through one black and massively swollen eye.

"Marshal," Felton said, slamming his newspaper down on his desk. "I'm going to ask you to leave right now. You have no business here and I really don't appreciate you hanging around."

"Is that a fact?"

"Sure is. You have your business to take care of and I have mine."

"And is your business beating up prisoners?" Longarm asked, his voice quiet but with a hard, threatening edge.

"What the hell are you talking about!"

Longarm saw naked fear on Hilda's face and . . . and a little hope at the sight of his unexpected arrival. The woman said nothing, but stared at him.

"Marshal Long," Felton said, coming toward him, "did you hear what I just told you? I said I want you to leave right now!"

Longarm turned and pushed off the bars. "What happened to your prisoner's eye, Dub?"

The sheriff stopped in his tracks, his own eyes jumping back and forth between Hilda and Longarm. "The bitch fell and hit her face on the bunk. Nasty bit of business, but it happens. I think someone managed to sneak a bottle through the window bars and Hilda got drunk and did that damage to herself."

"Hilda fell? Is that what you just said?"

"That's right!" Felton's lip curled. "Hilda, tell the man that is what happened to you."

Hilda didn't speak.

Longarm knew what had really happened to the young woman. He could see it in her eyes and he could see it in the nervous twitch at the corner of Dub Felton's mouth.

"Sheriff," Longarm said quietly, "I'd like to have a few quiet words with the prisoner."

"The hell you say!"

"The hell I *do* say. And while I'm doing that, I suggest that you go for a little walk. This won't take long and the fresh air will prove to be good for your health."

Dub Felton wasn't a small man in any sense of the word. He was at least six feet tall and weighed around two-twenty. And the sheriff was solid muscle. Longarm was sure that Sheriff Felton was a tough fighter who had probably not been whipped since he was a boy. Longarm also knew that he could take Felton. But kicking the Sacramento sheriff's ass in his own office would result in some serious consequences.

"Listen, Dub. I have a few questions to ask Hilda about her sister and the death of her father. Questions that I don't believe she will answer with you present. So why don't you just simmer down and give me a little time alone with Hilda rather than push us into something that neither of us wants to happen . . . if you catch my drift."

Longarm's reasonable tone and his words had the hoped-for effect. Felton had been given an out and a way to salvage his pride and he was eager to take both rather than fight.

"Well, all right, I'll do it as a professional courtesy but don't push it," he said, making it sound as if he were offering Longarm the biggest favor of his life. "I'll give you ten minutes alone with her. But if there is any problem or if you have some other gawdamn agenda in mind, believe me when I say I'll arrest you and you will spend time in that empty jail cell. Understood?"

"Perfectly."

"Okay then," Felton said, pivoting around, going to his hat rack and heading for the door. He turned at the last minute and made a big show of extracting his pocket watch, consulting it and then saying, "Ten minutes, Marshal Long. Not a minute more and then you aren't coming back here."

Longarm didn't bother to tell the lawman that he'd come back if he damn well chose to return . . . no point in saying that at all. So he just nodded and watched Dub Felton close the door and step outside.

The instant they were alone, Hilda flew off the bunk and grabbed the bars. "Custis, please! I can't stay here another night! He's hurting me! I'm bleeding inside and . . ."

Hilda Olsen began to sob.

"Pull up your dress," Longarm asked quietly, a powerful anger building deep in his stomach.

"What?"

"I just want to see what he did to you."

"Custis, I'm not wearing any undergarments," she said

in a trembling voice. "The sheriff took them after he raped me the first night."

"I have to see you, Hilda."

She drew her dress up to just below her belly button and when Longarm saw the teeth bites and the deep, purple bruises around her womanhood, a rage formed inside of him that was almost beyond his control.

"Drop it," he managed to whisper as he swung around and marched toward the door. "I'll be right back."

Sheriff Dub Felton was standing a few feet away on the boardwalk talking to several men. He was laughing and Longarm didn't hear the joke or the words and he didn't give Felton a chance.

"Gawddamn you!" he hissed. Longarm grabbed the Sacramento sheriff by the shoulder, spun him around, and buried his right fist in Felton's gut. The lawman's mouth formed a silent scream and Longarm followed his attack with a lashing left hook to Felton's mouth and nose that lifted the lawman completely off his feet.

"Hey!" one of the men that Felton had been talking to shouted. "What the hell are you doing!"

Longarm didn't bother to answer. Felton was bent over with blood pouring from his smashed lips and broken nose. Longarm grabbed the man's ears and drove his knee up into Felton's face, sending him off the boardwalk and onto his back.

"You son of a bitch!" Longarm shouted. "You've been raping and torturing Hilda!"

Felton's eyes were glazed as Longarm stepped off the boardwalk intending to grab the sheriff and beat what was left of his face into an unrecognizable and bloody mass.

But someone moved swiftly up behind him and when the

blow to the back of Longarm's head landed, he knew that it wasn't a fist . . . no, it was very hard . . . a club but more likely the barrel of a rifle or a gun.

After that, Longarm didn't even remember falling face-down into the street or being landed on by men and their flying fists and boots.

# Chapter 21

Longarm had been thrown into the cell next to Hilda and when he awoke, he felt as if his skull had been split down the center with the blade of an ax. He picked himself off the floor and staggered over to the metal bunk covered with a thin straw-filled mattress.

"Custis?"

Longarm glanced to his right through bars to see double visions of Hilda.

"Custis, are you going to be all right?"

"Probably . . . given some time."

"I heard that you beat Sheriff Felton half to death."

"I broke his nose and if I'd have had another shot at him I'd have broken his jaw," Longarm told her. "But someone must have bent a barrel across the back of my head."

There was a long silence before Hilda added, "When he comes back he's going to try to figure out a way to kill you."

Longarm reached back and gingerly touched his scalp and was not surprised to discover his hair was matted with dried blood. Whoever had struck him had done so with enough force and malice to kill. Double images of everything swam before his eyes and he felt dizzy so he bent forward and cradled his head in his hands and closed his eyes.

"Custis, did you hear what I said?"

"I think you said that Sheriff Felton . . ." He couldn't remember the rest.

"I said he will figure out a way to *kill* you," Hilda repeated.

Longarm tried to stand up, but when the world began to spin he sat back down on the bunk. The pain was intense and it was coming at him in rolling waves.

"We have to get out of here!" Hilda whispered, her voice carrying a desperation that was impossible to ignore.

Longarm took a couple of deep breaths. He felt like vomiting and the world would not stop spinning. "Hilda, I'm not capable of doing anything right now and I don't even think I can walk yet."

"You don't really know that man," Hilda pleaded. "You beat him up in front of everyone and he won't stand for that."

"In case you've forgotten, I'm a deputy United States marshal, and I don't care how vicious or vengeful the sheriff is . . . he can't get away with murdering me."

"You're terribly wrong," Hilda hissed. "They took your gun and your badge."

"Who are *they*?" Longarm managed to ask.

"They're the same ones that paid the sheriff to let them into my cell at night and rape me over and over."

Longarm was not sure he'd heard her correctly. He raised his head and shook it hard. "Are you saying that Felton was making money off you right here in this office last night?"

"That's right! Don't you believe me?"

Longarm massaged his temples hard with his thumbs. He took a few more deep breaths and the room slowed down to a slow spin. "I . . . I can't imagine that you'd make something up like that and I did see the damage when you lifted your skirt."

He pushed himself to his feet and staggered over to the bars to hang on to them in order to keep from falling. "Hilda, I believe you but Felton doesn't strike me as being stupid enough to try and murder a federal officer of the law."

"But he will because he can't let you tell anyone what he's had done to me at night. People think I'm a murderer and sure to hang for the death of Senator Baker so the sheriff can do pretty much whatever he wants to me and it won't matter. But you're a lawman and if you tell people what he's done in here, at least some of them will believe you and that will cause all kinds of problems for Sheriff Felton."

Longarm made himself concentrate. Hilda was convincing, and from what he'd seen of Felton, she might even be right.

"Let's assume that you're correct about Felton and that he is crazy enough to have me killed. How could he do that?"

"I don't know! But he *will*. Don't you understand that we've got to get out of here?"

Longarm reached out and touched Hilda's face, realizing that she was absolutely terrified and her fear got through to him. "Just try to calm yourself and I'll think of something."

"You'd better do it before Sheriff Felton gets back from the hospital."

"Jailbreak," Longarm heard himself say. "The only way that it could happen so that it looked believable to the public would be to stage a jailbreak, then gun us down. It's been done often enough before . . . even in a city as big as Sacramento. But what I'm wondering is if you're just saying this so that you can escape."

Hilda reached through the bars and touched his face with her soft fingers. "I can't get a fair trial here in Sacramento. In the eyes of the people, I'm guilty. I could see it the minute I arrived in the faces of everyone. I'll be sentenced to hang and of that there is little doubt."

"I overheard someone tell Felton that the judge, a man named Gratton, had to suddenly leave town and travel to San Diego to help his sick mother and that he might not return for quite some time."

"It doesn't matter when he returns," Hilda said quietly. "Because by then, we'll *both* be dead."

A sharp stab of pain sent Longarm staggering back to the bunk where he sat down heavily. "Let me rest for a while and think this through," he told her. "Maybe I can get someone to send a telegram to Marshal Vail in Denver. He'll make sure that we aren't murdered. He'll see we get help."

"By the time he could get here with help, it will be too late. We're on our own and I don't have any idea of what to do, and I can't bear to have them rape me again tonight."

Turning his head to look at Hilda, Longarm had a feeling that every word she'd told him was going to come true unless he figured out some way to get out of this jail . . . and do it fast.

Ten minutes later, two men barged into the office and sauntered up to the cells. Longarm was pretty sure they had been talking to the sheriff when he'd burst outside and beaten the local lawman so swiftly that no one had the time to intervene until the damage had already been inflicted.

"So," the largest of the pair crowed, "we've come to see if you're still alive. Looks like you are, which is a gawdamn shame. I thought I hit you hard enough to either kill you or make you a slobbering idiot."

Longarm raised his head and stared through the bars at the leering man. "What's your name?"

The big man hadn't been expecting a question and it took him a moment to lose his sneer and say, "Frank. Frank Lowe. What the hell does it matter?"

"I just wanted to know," Longarm said. "For later."

Lowe had a round, beefy face and a full beard with deep-set eyes. His clothes were filthy and his big shoulders were humped like the back of a bull buffalo. He grinned, displaying a set of tobacco-stained teeth. "You know, Marshal, the cell keys are hanging over there on a wall hook and I've half a mind to get 'em and finish the job I left undone outside."

Longarm studied his big fists a moment and then managed a thin smile. "I think that's a fine idea, Frank. And while you're at it why don't you invite your friend to join in."

The smaller man took a quick step back. "I didn't touch you out there and I ain't interested in doing you any harm now. My name is Will Goshen and I don't want a thing to do with you."

"Then," Longarm said, "you're far brighter than your friend. Did you both pay the sheriff to rape Hilda Olsen the last couple of nights?"

The question had its desired effect. Goshen began to shake his head furiously. His eyes darted from Longarm to Hilda and he blurted, "You can ask her. I didn't pay for it last night or any other night. Not from that woman or any other. I got a gal of my own named Trudy and we're going to be married next year."

Longarm glanced at Hilda, who nodded, telling him that the smaller man was telling the truth. "I'm glad to hear that," Longarm said. "And if I were you, Goshen, I'd light out of here and stay as far away from this place as you can. Nothing good is going to come of being here and I'm not going to forget someone who wronged me . . . not ever."

Goshen looked deep into Longarm's eyes and without a word turned and left.

"He's a scared little rabbit," Lowe said with contempt.

Longarm walked unsteadily across his cell. "You paid the sheriff to rape Hilda, didn't you."

It wasn't a question and Longarm didn't have to look over to Hilda to know that he had guessed it right.

"She was good and I reamed her a bigger hole."

Longarm smiled weakly. "Why don't you go over there and get those keys and come inside?"

Lowe's eyes settled on Hilda in the next cell and he swallowed hard. "Dub won't be coming around until evening. I could use a little of the woman right now. You, I can finish after I ride her."

"Finish me off first," Longarm said with a wolfish grin. "Or show yourself to be the coward you really are, Frank."

The big man stepped back. "What do I tell Dub and the others when they come in and find your blood all over the floor and your head caved in?"

"Tell them that when I went wild you tried to shut me up and when I wouldn't listen you came inside and had to kill me with your fists."

Longarm shrugged as if it were the simplest and most reasonable explanation in the world. "Because if I watch you rape Hilda again, I'll tell everyone what I saw and that could go real bad for you."

Frank Lowe rubbed his thick beard. He was thinking hard and when his eyes settled on the cowering Hilda and raked her body, that seemed to make his decision. "I could have her now and not have to pay Dub a thing for it," he reasoned out loud.

"What about me first?" Longarm asked.

"I'd like killing you about as much as fucking her again."

"Then you should stop talking and do both before Sheriff Felton comes back from the doctor's office or the hospital. Once he returns, you'll have to pay for the woman."

"Yeah, Dub sure as hell would make me pay for it again."

"Then get the cell keys and let's see how tough you really are, Frank. Or would you rather show the yellow stripe up your back that marks you as a coward?"

Frank went to get the keys while Longarm started breathing in and out hard, trying to get back his strength and regain some clear focus. He had perhaps a minute before the big man started beating on him with the intent to kill. One minute to gather whatever he had left inside and put up a fight to the finish.

It was going to be an uphill battle, a high mountain that he must climb or he was a dead man and Hilda was in for a hellish time that just might send her mind flying right over the edge and into the dark abyss of insanity.

He looked around for something . . . anything to use as a weapon and found nothing. But then he realized that while they'd taken his gun belt, they had not taken his waist belt and its buckle. Longarm unbuckled the belt. It wasn't much, but it might just give him the edge in this fight that he so desperately needed given his dizziness and temporary physical weakness.

# Chapter 22

Lowe selected a large key and inserted it into Longarm's cell door, turning it slowly, his eyes never leaving those of his unsteady and intended victim. When the door swung open he stuffed the long cell key into his pocket, leaving the ring and several other keys dangling at his side.

"This is going to be good," he said, balling his fists. "I ain't touched you yet and you're still wobbly on your feet."

Longarm wished his unsteadiness was an act, but unfortunately it wasn't. The dizziness had returned and he started blinking fast trying to correct his double vision.

Suddenly, Frank Lowe rushed across the tight space. Longarm raised his hands to block the overhand right with the intention of slamming a left uppercut into Lowe's gut. But the deputy's overhand came in so fast and hard that he never had a chance and lights behind his eyes exploded like red rockets. He hit the floor and rolled, knowing that Lowe would use his boots with devastating effect. Longarm threw himself under the metal cot and Lowe kicked it with his shin, striking the hard edge of the metal. He screamed in pain. Longarm grabbed the man's ankle and yanked with all of his strength. Lowe hit the floor with a loud grunt and Longarm tried to garrote the man with his belt, but he was far too weak to hold the powerful deputy down. Rising to his knees, Lowe punched out again and again and Longarm felt himself losing consciousness as his head snapped back and forth with each punishing blow.

Knowing he had to get away, Longarm crabbed frantically toward the next cell, dimly hearing Hilda's shouts. Lowe landed on his back like a ton of rocks, grabbed fistfuls of Longarm's hair, and started to jerk his head backward.

Suddenly, Lowe released his grip and screamed, "Ahhh!"

Longarm rolled the man off him and realized that Hilda had his belt's buckle in her hands and had jammed its two-inch long metal prong deep into the deputy's right eye. Lowe's head was flung back and he was howling in agony. Longarm somehow managed to climb to his hands and knees, desperate to use this moment to his advantage, knowing that if he failed Lowe would kill him.

"Custis!"

Longarm raised his head just in time to get his belt thrown through the bars into his face. "Strangle him now!"

Deputy Frank Lowe was staggering around in circles with his head tilted back and blood pouring from his blinded eye. Longarm whipped his belt around Lowe's ankles and yanked the man down hard. The air gushed out of his lungs as he fell flat on his stomach. Longarm crawled up on top of the screaming deputy, wrapped the belt around Lowe's bull neck and with his teeth bared and the muscles of his arms knotted, he twisted the belt and threw all his weight backward.

Lowe's neck snapped and his head flopped sideways as if it had been severed. Longarm felt the man's body jerk and buck for a few moments before a long sigh escaped Lowe's mouth and the deputy shuddered his way into hell. Longarm collapsed on the dead man, feeling as if his lungs were on fire while his head whirled like a dervish.

"Custis, don't pass out! Get the keys and unlock my cell!"

Longarm rolled off Lowe's body and using his elbows and knees managed to drag himself out of his cell. Somehow, he hauled himself up on the cell door and then, hanging onto the bars, worked his way around to Hilda's cell and got it unlocked.

She burst out of the cell, grabbed Longarm before he could collapse, and helped him over to Sheriff Felton's desk chair.

"We did it," she breathed, face wild with happiness and relief. "Custis, we did it!"

Longarm started breathing in and out fast again and nearly folded over and crashed headlong to the floor. At the last instant, Hilda grabbed and pushed him erect. "We have to go!"

"I can't," he confessed. "I don't think I can even walk right now."

She slapped his cheeks, and not gently. When he didn't rouse enough, Hilda tore open one of the drawers. "Dub keeps his bottle here. I watched."

A moment later, she was prying open Longarm's mouth and pouring whiskey down his throat. It was *bad* whiskey and it burned like fire but it had the desired and stimulating effect. Longarm choked and grabbed the bottle and took a few more gulps as his mind sharpened and his single vision returned.

"That's enough for now," Hilda said, extracting the bottle from his hands, taking a swallow and then tossing it aside. "We've got to get out of here quick because someone is bound to show up."

"My gun and holster," Longarm muttered, vaguely pointing to a wall peg.

Hilda collected his gun and holster and also grabbed a rifle and a pistol for herself. She made sure that they were loaded and then she helped Longarm to his feet.

"I'll stand by the door and when it's clear, we make a dash to the right for an alley between this building and the next. We keep moving until we put some distance between us and this jail."

"Where can we hide?" he asked, not even trying to think ahead to what would happen when it was discovered that he had strangled Deputy Lowe to death in his cell.

"I know lots of places," she said. "But there is one place that they'd never think to look that is close and secluded."

"Where is that?"

"Senator Baker's home," she said. "Most likely it is locked up and empty. And if it's not, we'll just have to do whatever is necessary."

He looked at her closely. "Are you sure that . . ."

"If we can just stay free for a day or two, we can figure out how to leave Sacramento alive."

Longarm knew this was all wrong. He should stay and explain to someone of authority how Frank Lowe and Sheriff Felton had raped Hilda and abused her terribly and then why he'd been forced to fight for his life.

But who in this town would believe him? They'd already been certain that Hilda and Pearl were murderers . . . and maybe they were. But now . . . until he could think clearly enough to figure things out . . . Longarm knew that he would also be branded a murder.

Lynch mob justice seemed a very ugly inevitability.

"Okay," he said, buckling on his gun belt and taking slow, measured steps toward the door. "When it's clear to go, we'll make a run for it and sort things out later."

"There's nothing to sort out," she said, opening the front door a crack with one hand while holding a gun in the other. "This is the law of the jungle and we're the prey."

Longarm remembered his badge. He managed to make his way back to Felton's desk and retrieve it, then he rejoined Hilda.

"Can you move fast?" she asked, studying him anxiously.

"Hell no."

"I could leave you and better my chances."

Longarm unholstered his gun and cocked back the hammer. "If you try," he warned, "I'd have to kill you because, as far as I'm concerned, you're still my prisoner."

Hilda almost laughed and then she pushed the door open, took his free hand and they began to run like hunted animals . . . like prey.

# Chapter 23

Pearl Olsen had sold the medicine wagon, horse, harness, and its elixir, then used part of the money to buy first-class train tickets to Bent's Fort where she caught the Atchison, Topeka and Santa Fe Railroad and rode it all the way to Los Angeles. With luck and good timing she made a swift connection on the Southern Pacific, and with her hair dyed black she disembarked in Oakland and caught the daily passenger steamer to Sacramento, arriving to learn that her sister and the marshal from Denver had killed a deputy just six days earlier and were the subjects of a huge manhunt.

Aware that any attractive woman always drew a lot of looks and attention, Pearl found an upscale whorehouse where she'd never worked and had men lining up, panting to ravish her lovely body. She needed to refresh her finances, but even more she wanted to hear the constant news concerning the manhunt of her sister and the United States federal marshal.

A short, ugly man in his fifties but with more vigor than

she had thought imaginable grunted and then shrilled in ecstasy as he reached his climax and then rolled over gasping for breath that would not come.

"Shit a-fire, Wilbur, you aren't going to *die* here in bed, are you!"

"Damn, that was good and if I have to die, I'd like it to be between your lovely legs."

"You're a *real* man," she said, grabbing a bottle of good whiskey and taking a long pull. "You may not look it, but you've got what it takes to satisfy any woman."

"Really?" Wilbur beamed and looked down at his dying erection. "I guess I do pretty good for a man my size and age."

"You're amazing, Wilbur."

"Coming from a woman with your looks and body, I'm feeling like I'm walking in the clouds right now."

"Here," Pearl said, "have some of this expensive whiskey I keep for only the best men I service because you're pale and if your ticker quit with me I'd lose this job."

"The way you look and fuck, you could work at a lot classier places than this," Wilbur said, stroking her nearest breast, "but then I probably couldn't afford the price of you."

"You got that one right. You were telling me about that jailbreak and murder."

"Oh, yeah," Wilbur said, rolling over to adoringly gaze at Pearl. "This woman, Hilda Olsen, who murdered Senator Baker a month or so ago, was delivered to our jail by this big Denver marshal. Anyway . . ." Wilbur lost his train of thought and tried to put his finger into Pearl but she slapped his busy little hand away.

"You've already got more than your three dollar's worth," Pearl snapped, getting off the bed and squatting over a pail to scrub away his pitiful few drops of seed. She reached for a dry towel and finished the job before asking, "So now you've got me curious. Are you telling that there is this big manhunt and they haven't found the pair?"

"It's not just a manhunt," Wilbur corrected. "It's also a *womanhunt*. And while I didn't get to see the murderess, everyone said she was beautiful . . . but I'm sure not as pretty as you."

"So where are the lawmen looking?"

Wilburn motioned for the bottle of whiskey in Pearl's hand. "I understand they're watching the railroad depot and all the stage lines out of town. Packets and ships going downriver to San Francisco, too, but so far, nothing. They've also sent posses north and south along the Sierras . . . but no luck."

"Then," Pearl mused, "the pair must still be right here in Sacramento."

Wilbur shrugged. "Mind if I have another pull on your bottle?"

"As a matter of fact I do. You're time is up, Wilbur. Get dressed and get out."

Wilbur's expression looked hurt and then he pouted. "I thought you liked me . . . a little anyway. I got some money saved for retirement. And a nice little house on Sutter Street . . . one of the best parts of town. I am an important man in this community and have many friends. Big bank account and a prosperous business. I'm an attorney, you know."

Pearl had an idea. "You say you own a nice house and you're a lawyer?"

"That's right. My wife died a few years ago and . . ."

"Oh," Pearl said, suddenly looking concerned. "I'm *really* sorry."

Wilbur's lower lip trembled and he sniffled. "Ethel was a fine woman, but she was always frail and we never had any children. I get lonesome and I may be short and fat and not much to look at, but there are women in this town who would marry me."

"I'm sure that they would."

"As you've just learned, I'm all man and I can still satisfy a woman. But most of them in Sacramento that want to be with me are spinsters . . . wrinkled old bags just after my house and money."

Pearl nodded sympathetically. "A man in your position has to be very careful and people can be very cruel."

"I know," Wilbur said. "You wouldn't believe the things I hear at my office. Some people are terrible and have had hard, bitter lives."

"I'm one of them," Pearl confessed in a small voice. "As just a little girl I was constantly raped by my own father and brothers."

His jaw fell and then he clamped it shut and leaned closer, fists clenched in anger. "Really?"

It was the truth and Pearl had no trouble saying, "Really. I was destined to live a life of shame and moral degradation."

"I'm so sorry."

"Me, too," Pearl said, wiping a nonexistent tear from her eye. "Men have always just wanted me for their pleasure, not realizing I have a heart and real feelings despite the rocky road of life that I have had to take."

"I can see that," Wilbur said, reaching for his pants and bringing out his wallet. "Could we just . . . just talk and have a few drinks together right here in this room? I'll pay you for your time and maybe I'll be ready to do it again with you before long."

Pearl saw the thick wad of money in Wilbur's wallet. She smiled sweetly and removed her silk gown, then lay back on the bed, legs spread just slightly. Wilbur gulped and snuggled down beside her then slipped his little finger into her womanhood.

"Oh my gosh," he breathed, "I think I've died and gone to heaven."

"Not quite," she whispered, reaching for his puckered little pecker with the idea of somehow stroking it back to liveliness and then finding herself another sucker to milk bone-dry.

# Chapter 24

Longarm paced restlessly back and forth in Senator Baker's impressive library while Hilda sat on the sofa reading a beautifully leather-bound book on Roman weapons of war. "Hilda, I have to get a telegram to Billy Vail in Denver."

She looked up and gently shook her head. "Custis, we both have agreed that, if you go to the telegraph office, you'll be spotted immediately. You're such a tall, handsome, and broad-shouldered man that everyone will recognize you the minute you appear in public."

Longarm scowled, knowing she was right. And with her long blond hair and exceptional looks, Hilda would be quickly identified. He sat back down in a leather chair and sipped his drink, thinking hard about how they could get out of this fix.

"I'm sorry you're so upset and fidgety," Hilda offered after a few minutes. "This is the perfect hiding place and we've everything here we could ever want. Good food, good whiskey, and even champagne. There are enough books in this library to occupy us for years."

"You're right about all that," Longarm agreed, "but sooner or later, someone is going to come in here after realizing it is the perfect place for us to hide out, and they'll come in force with guns in hand."

"If they do, we hide and they'll never find us. This mansion is huge and I know of some secret places. I don't see why you are so impatient and can't just enjoy spending a week or two here."

"Because," Longarm explained, "I'm not a man for sitting around when misguided people with ropes in their hands are intent on catching and stringing us up from a tree limb."

"Well, I don't know quite what to say," Hilda told him with exasperation surfacing in her voice. "You told me that every stage line and steamboat was no doubt being watched and it would be insane to try and buy a ticket on the railroad back over the Sierras. So what can we do as long as there is a big manhunt going on for us?"

"We'll have to leave and get everything straightened out sooner or later."

Hilda laid her book down and came to sit beside him. "Custis, if we're too impatient and get caught because of it, you've already told me that there is a high likelihood that we'll be lynched on the spot without the hope of a fair trial."

"That's true."

"So," Hilda continued, "even if you see me as your prisoner, you have to be mindful that it is *my* life as well as your own that hangs in the balance of this decision. I've never seen a hanging, but I can well imagine how horrible it is . . . especially if you are the one dropping through the trapdoor or being pulled up choking and kicking while desperately trying to grab and loosen the noose around your neck."

"Hilda, I've had to witness a good many hangings and I remember every one of them in great detail; sometimes they come to me in the middle of the night and I sit up in a cold sweat. It doesn't matter if the condemned deserved to be hanged or not . . . it's still a terrible way to die."

"I'm sorry those memories haunt you, Custis. But I still believe that we should hide out here a few more days and nights," she said coming over to sit beside him. "And since you are so tense about all of this, I feel we should retire to the senator's bedroom and see if we can get you *relaxed*."

Longarm almost laughed out loud. "Hilda," he said, "you are quite a character."

She leaned over and nibbled on his ear then slipped her hands down his flat stomach. "Why don't we just enjoy ourselves while we have this chance? Three days from now . . . maybe a week or even a month and we might be rotting at the end of a rope."

He stared at her. "That's a hell of a thing to say or think about."

"But true." Hilda stood and began to undress. "Maybe we should make love right here on this colorful and lovely Persian rug. Wouldn't you like that?"

Longarm leaned back and watched her undress. He tossed down his whiskey and felt his manhood grow with anticipation. "Hilda, you are quite the temptress."

Hilda finished undressing and found a pillow from the couch. She placed it on the beautiful rug and then lay down with a mischievous grin on her lovely face. "Custis, come and make love to me and stop worrying about tomorrow."

He nodded in agreement, saying, "Right now I'm clay in your hands, woman."

"You're a lot harder than clay. Come on, honey. Let's not waste time over things we can't yet control. All we're lacking right now is a roaring fire and a bearskin rug but we can make do with the Persian, don't you think?"

Longarm knew that he could "make do" with this situation just fine. He quickly undressed, then knelt down beside Hilda and kissed her lips.

"Now you're getting into the spirit," Hilda whispered, her hand stroking his manhood. "Old Senator Baker used to like to do this right here where we're lying."

Longarm started with surprise. "You and him coupled often on this rug?"

"Yes, of course. I loved Taft and he loved me. At first, I thought of him as just an old fool who had a beautiful home and lots of money to lavish on me and Pearl. But after a while, my feelings changed and although I was never passionately in love with the man, I came to admire him and I wanted to give the senator comfort from his physical problems and also real pleasure. He was a fine man, Custis."

"And what did your sister think of the senator?"

In response to the question, Hilda's strong fingers tightened on Longarm's manhood, but then slowly eased their pressure. "Let's not talk about Pearl or the senator right now. Let's not talk about anything."

Hilda rolled away and took a position on her hands and knees. "Take me from behind this time. And while you're doing it, wrap your hand around my hips and use your finger to touch me where it feels so heavenly."

Longarm moved around behind the beautiful woman. Hilda had a lovely bottom and he playfully kissed each of her butt cheeks before he entered her from the rear. She moaned and he wrapped his arms around her hips and found her source of greatest pleasure.

"Slowly," she breathed, head down, long blond hair hanging around her face and tendrils touching the rug. "Nice and easy and slow."

Longarm knew how to do that and as his finger worked her little nub of desire, his manhood moved in and out of Hilda until they were both straining wildly in a burst of sexual satisfaction.

When it was over, Hilda rolled onto her back and stared up at the high ceiling, seemingly lost in her own thoughts.

"What are you thinking?" Longarm asked.

"Oh, I'm not sure I should tell you."

"Are you remembering when you did this with the senator?"

She sighed. "However did you guess?"

"Tell me what he was like other than that he was a great man."

Hilda pursed her lips for a moment, then said, "He was gentle but strong and very wise. Taft was also a self-made man. His family owned a dairy and he worked from dawn to dusk as a boy."

Longarm pointed up at the stacks of leather-bound books. "He must have been quite well educated and intellectual."

"He was," Hilda agreed. "But despite his wealth and fame, Taft wasn't a very happy man and I could never figure out exactly why. He had no children and that was part of his sense of loss and his wife had died. He had become moody and temperamental . . . and he had a sudden, terrible temper."

"Did he beat or abuse you or Pearl?"

"No, but Taft could inflict his most devastating punishment in the form of words and he did it often to Pearl. I was his favorite and I'm quite sure that he thought of me as something between a wife and a daughter . . . and his friend. But the senator sensed that my twin sister was stronger and angrier than myself and so he constantly tried to beat Pearl down and make her feel small and dirty. He knew of her past and he never let her forgot her mistakes."

"So," Longarm mused, "did Pearl finally lose her temper and murder him?"

Hilda didn't answer but instead rose to her feet and reached for the bottle and her empty glass. "Custis, we should talk about something else."

"I need to know if Pearl killed the senator all on her own."

"I'm sorry but I'm never going to put a noose around my sister's neck."

"Even if it might mean saving your own neck?"

Hilda stared down at Longarm, who was still lying naked on the Persian rug. "Custis, I've never seen a man with so many scars. And although I've asked you about a few of the most prominent ones, I'm sure there are many that have their own interesting stories."

"Unimportant history," he told her, coming to his feet.

"And so is what happened in this room and in Senator Baker's many bedrooms."

Longarm raised his glass to her. "I have to say I've never enjoyed being with a prisoner charged with murder as much as I've enjoyed being with you."

"And I've never been under arrest for murder and had so much fun."

They drank and then Longarm paused to consider his next words. "Hilda, if you tell me that you had no part in the murder of Senator Taft Baker, I'll believe you and even more importantly, I'll do whatever I can to see that you are rid forever of the charges of murder that you are now facing."

"You would do that for me?

"Yes, I would."

"But in exchange I'd have to tell you that my twin sister murdered the senator. Isn't that right? And if I did that, I'm not sure that I could ever live with myself."

Longarm shook his head, not understanding. "For the life of me I can't understand what hold Pearl has on you."

Hilda swilled her drink, eyes focused on the amber liquor in her glass for a moment before she answered. "Pearl always looked out for and protected me even though we were the same size and age. She was just tougher and my family understood that she had something dark in her that was dangerous and should not be tested. Once, when I was frolicking in a pond and my brother sneaked up and then jumped on me intending to rape me, Pearl heard my screams. I'll never forget the look on her face or the mossy rock in her hand that she used to nearly brain my brother. Pa didn't punish Pearl for doing that; we were fourteen and it was the first time that I realized he was actually afraid of my twin sister."

"I see."

"Pearl was my best friend and protector for a lot of terrible years during my childhood. We never fought because I knew I could never win. She has a . . . a hardness and a spirit that will never be broken. If she walks the gallows, she will spit in the hangman's eye and laugh at the crowd before she swings. She's like no one else I know and I love her for that."

"Even though she is a murderess?"

"She has always been more of a savior to me," Hilda said quietly.

"So," Longarm said, "we've come full circle and I still don't have the answers to the most important questions surrounding the death of Senator Baker."

"True," Hilda admitted, "but we've just made wild and passionate love on a very expensive Persian rug and that's not something to be easily dismissed or quickly forgotten . . . is it?"

"No, Hilda," he heard himself say, "it most certainly is not."

# Chapter 25

It had taken Pearl Olsen just fifteen minutes of searching Wilbur's house to find out where he hid his jewelry and cash. It wasn't a huge haul because the lawyer had told her he kept most of his valuables in a bank's safety-deposit box and his cash in a Wells Fargo account. But there was a gold watch and chain and a fine emerald ring to be taken along with almost two hundred dollars.

Pearl had tried to think of some way to force Wilbur to empty his bank box account, but the risk of being arrested in the attempt was too great so she settled on a simple household theft. No doubt, when Wilbur discovered she had robbed him, he would be so humiliated that he would not even file a report.

Only this morning had she finally realized that the one place that the authorities would not think to look for the Denver marshal and her twin sister would be Senator Baker's empty mansion. So with her hair still dyed black and wearing a frumpy coat that made her look like a poor housekeeper,

Pearl knew that no one would even come close to recognizing her. As Pearl neared the senator's impressive two-story mansion her footsteps slowed and she stood on the corner of the street looking up and down to make sure that no one was watching. Satisfied, Pearl slipped around behind the mansion and through the trees to a small carriage house. She checked the door and found it locked. but she did notice that someone had recently been in the senator's backyard.

Pearl patted the six-gun strapped to her shapely hip. There was no point in waiting until nightfall to enter the mansion and then creep from room to room checking to see if Hilda and Marshal Long were asleep. No, her impatience to extract vengeance against the Denver marshal was too great to allow any hesitation. And besides, Pearl knew this home like the back of her hand and so she removed her shoes and crept up to the door leading into the kitchen. The door appeared to have been forced open and that made her heart quicken with anticipation.

Someone was here!

Pearl eased the door open and stepped inside, unholstering the six-shot Colt revolver. She tiptoed into the dim kitchen and paused to listen. She heard voices that had to be coming from the library. Pearl took a deep breath and began to creep down the hallway with the voices growing louder and then she heard her sister cry out. Pearl almost jumped into the library, but then she realized that she had also heard a man's groan of sexual release like the ones she'd heard so many times in whorehouses.

They are fucking!

A cold smile played across Pearl's face and she pushed through the door to see her naked sister and the marshal sprawled across the senator's big leather sofa. Hilda's bare chest was heaving and the man was just pulling his rod out of her when Pearl cocked back the hammer of her pistol and asked, "Having fun?"

Longarm's head swiveled toward the voice and then he started to reach for his Colt revolver, but Pearl fired and Longarm's left hand turned to liquid fire; it was all he could do not to scream. The bullet had plowed through the hand and blood was flowing freely so he made a fist, hoping that would stanch the flow. The pain was so intense he could hardly hold a thought, much less think of a way to save his and Hilda's lives.

"Next one is going to blow off that big thing between your legs, Marshal. I can't miss at this distance so I'd advise you to sit down beside my sister and don't say a word. Hilda, tidy up your bottom and cover yourself with a pillow. You're here fucking the man that killed our father, Aunt Edna, and our brothers, and it makes me sick to my stomach."

Hilda grabbed a pillow and placed it over herself. "Pearl, what . . ."

"Don't say a word yet," Pearl warned, the barrel of her gun moving back and forth between her sister and Longarm. "I'm going to do the talking."

Pearl walked over to a nearby chair and settled into it. "I finally figured out that this was the only place in Sacramento that you'd be safe to hide in and I didn't waste any time getting here. But now, Hilda, the question is, what am I going to do with you because one of us has to die. It's the only way that the other can be free and have a chance to start over."

Hilda's face turned white. "You'd kill me? You'd kill your *own sister*?"

Pearl shrugged. "You're the one that took up with a

lawman. What else can I do? Whatever happens next is because you brought it on all by yourself."

"I never meant for our family men to be killed . . . never meant it at all," Hilda rushed. "It . . . it all just spiraled out of control."

Pearl shook her head. "You were always the needy one and I was always the strong one. I guess after today, I won't have to worry about taking care of my weak sister anymore."

Longarm felt his mouth go dry but managed to say, "You say you're the strong one but what you really are is the one without a heart or soul. And you're the one who murdered Senator Baker, a man who took you and Hilda into his home and . . ."

"And made us do things to him that you can't even imagine," Pearl said, her voice harsh. "The senator was no saint, and he got about what he deserved when we shot him."

"We?" Longarm asked, taken by surprise and glancing at Hilda to see if this was the truth.

"Custis, I *did* shoot Taft but only because Pearl made me after she'd already stabbed him to death."

"Damn you, Hilda, you murdered the senator just the same as I did!"

Longarm cleared his throat. "Pearl, you are smart enough to know that you can't murder someone who is already dead."

"Why don't you just tie us up and go away?" Hilda asked. "We won't tell anyone you were here."

Pearl laughed coldly. "Even if I were stupid enough to believe you would never tell, your lawman lover wouldn't keep his silence."

Longarm's teeth were clenched in pain and he understood this evil woman was playing out her deadly game. Pearl wanted him to grovel for his life. Well, that was just not going to happen.

"Speak up, lawman!" Pearl shouted, cocking back the hammer of the pistol and aiming it at Longarm's exposed crotch. "I asked you a question and I expect an answer!"

"What you can expect and very soon," Longarm told the woman, "is a noose around your neck or a bullet in your brain. Your days are numbered and you'll never live long enough to see the inside of a prison."

Pearl studied him for a moment and then she aimed the pistol at Longarm's head.

"No!" Hilda cried, stepping in front of Longarm and holding out her hands in supplication.

"Get out of the way, Hilda, or I'll kill you first because, like I already said, one of us has to die."

"All your life you've protected me. I can't believe that you'd just shoot me down like this. We love each other, Pearl!"

"That's true," Pearl admitted. "But I love *my* life far more than I love *your* life and so this is the way it ends. We had some good times but a whole lot more bad ones."

Hilda suddenly threw herself at her sister just as the gun went off. Longarm saw blood spray from her head and he shoved Hilda down, leaping over her to knock Pearl sprawling. The gun flew from her hand and Longarm didn't bother trying to reach it but instead balled up his left hand and smashed Pearl in the chest, missing her throat.

Pearl rolled away, knocking over a table as she scrambled to reach the pistol. Longarm was on top of the woman in an instant.

A cry not unlike that of a soul being cast down into hell gushed out of Pearl's mouth and she grabbed Longarm's hair and bit his cheek, tearing off flesh. Longarm pried her away with an elbow and pounded her with his fists and didn't stop until Pearl's face was a ghoulish mix of blood, dyed black hair, and glistening white bone.

# Chapter 26

"Hilda!" he shouted, crawling over to her and seeing the blood that was seeping from her head wound. She was conscious, her blue eyes wide open and her bare chest heaving as if she had been running for a long time.

Longarm gently rolled her head to one side and with his index finger traced the path of Pearl's bullet, realizing with a huge sense of relief that the wound was just a shallow groove across her temple. "Hilda, you're going to make it," he said simply, as he found his shirt, tore off a bandage, and began to wrap a bandage around her head to stop the bleeding. "I'm going to get us dressed and to the hospital."

Hilda gripped his arm, unwilling to turn her head toward her sister. "What about . . ."

"She's dead."

Hilda bit her lower lip and tears rolled down her cheeks. "Pearl really did love and protect me, Custis. She never stopped."

"I'm sorry to tell you this, but she did stop," Longarm

countered. "Your twin sister was about to kill us both and would have if you hadn't thrown yourself forward and taken the bullet meant for me. Now I'm the one that's going to take care of you, not Pearl."

"Promise?" She squeezed his arm even tighter. "Promise you won't let them hang me?"

"I promise," Longarm vowed, voice thick with emotion.

Hilda reached up and hugged him. "I'm so afraid, Custis."

"It's going to be all right. I heard Pearl confess to stabbing the senator to death and . . ."

"But I shot him!"

"*He was already dead!* And anyway, let's just keep that part to ourselves. Do you understand what I'm telling you?"

"I do."

Longarm kissed Hilda before he picked her up and carried her upstairs to the bedroom they'd been using. "I've changed my mind about taking you to a hospital," he said. "Instead, I'm getting us out of Sacramento tonight."

"But . . ."

"Let me worry about it," Longarm interrupted. "I'm going to clean this mess up and you are going to change your name. I'll find you a new place to live far away from here and make sure that no one ever comes looking for you."

"How can you possibly do that?"

"I'm thinking on it right now."

"You should see a doctor right away, Custis. That wound to your hand is pretty awful."

"I've been hurt far worse. We need to get out of this town, and I know a place where there are people who will hide and help you. They happen to owe me some favors . . . rather large ones in fact."

Longarm got them both dressed. His hand was throbbing

and it hurt like hell, but the bullet had passed through cleanly and he could still move all his fingers. "I'll be back soon," he promised at the bedroom door. "And before tomorrow's dawn we'll be safe."

"I love you," Hilda whispered. "And I know you'll take care of me."

"I'll be back in an hour . . . two at the most."

Longarm had never stolen a buggy and horse but that night he did so without reservations. He noted the name of the livery and would send the owner more than enough money to compensate for his loss. And as promised, he was back at Hilda's side less than two hours later in the dark of the evening.

"We'll need blankets and some food," he told her. "Can you help gather up some things to hold us over for a week or so?"

"Of course. My head hurts and I feel a little weak, but I know where the picnic basket is kept and also some of the canned goods."

"Don't forget to add medicines and whiskey. Plenty of both."

"Where are we going?"

"I'll tell you later."

They were in the buggy and rolling south down California's great Central Valley by the morning's dawn. The fertile and huge valley country was covered with wildflowers and fields of crops. There were hundreds of prosperous farms and clear, bold rivers tumbling off the western slopes of the Sierra Nevadas.

Hilda sat close to Longarm. "This is such beautiful country!"

"It is," Longarm agreed. "I'd always wanted to see it."

Her eyes widened with surprise. "You mean that you've never been here before?"

"We're not staying in this part of California," he told her. "We're just sightseeing until we hit the southern end of the Sierras and then we'll travel up the eastern slope past a dead lake and then into a valley filled with grass and pines. I've friends there that own a big cattle ranch beside the Walker River. You're going to love it and it's not all that far south of Virginia City and Carson City."

"Will you please stay with me?" she dared to ask.

"I can't," he said with genuine regret. "My boss and his bosses are on their way to Sacramento, and I've got to go back there and set the record straight about why I had to kill that son of a bitch Frank Lowe and how I heard Pearl make a confession about murdering the senator, and then how I managed to . . . to kill her with my fists."

"What will you say when they ask you where I am?"

Longarm chuckled to himself. "I confess that I haven't figured that one out just quite yet."

She linked her arm through his and smelled the dark, rich soil waiting for spring to be turned by the plow, and the wildflowers that bloomed all across the great, warm valley.

"Custis, I wish that I could freeze time and we could stay just like this forever."

And without even thinking about it, Longarm nodded and heard himself say, "Me, too."

Watch for

**LONGARM AND THE SHARPSHOOTER**

the 431$^{st}$ novel in the exciting LONGARM
series from Jove

*Coming in October!*

## GIANT-SIZED ADVENTURE FROM AVENGING ANGEL LONGARM.

# BY TABOR EVANS

penguin.com/actionwesterns

M456AS0812

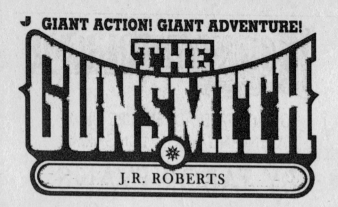

GIANT ACTION! GIANT ADVENTURE!

# THE GUNSMITH

## J.R. ROBERTS

penguin.com/actionwesterns

M455AS0812

DON'T MISS A YEAR OF

# Slocum Giant
by
# Jake Logan

**Slocum Giant 2004:**
**Slocum in the Secret**
**Service**

**Slocum Giant 2005:**
**Slocum and the Larcenous**
**Lady**

**Slocum Giant 2006:**
**Slocum and the Hanging**
**Horse**

**Slocum Giant 2007:**
**Slocum and the Celestial**
**Bones**

**Slocum Giant 2008:**
**Slocum and the Town**
**Killers**

**Slocum Giant 2009:**
**Slocum's Great**
**Race**

**Slocum Giant 2010:**
**Slocum Along**
**Rotten Row**

**Slocum Giant 2013:**
**Slocum and the Silver**
**City Harlot**

penguin.com/actionwesterns

M457AS0812

Jove Westerns put the "wild"
back into the Wild West

**LONGARM**
by Tabor Evans

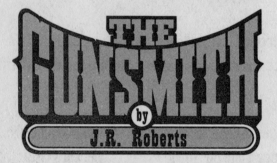

**THE GUNSMITH**
by
J.R. Roberts

**SLOCUM** by
**JAKE LOGAN**

Don't miss these exciting, all-action series!
penguin.com/actionwesterns

3 2953 01179939 4

M11G0610